THE PARABLE OF THE BLIND

Also by Gert Hofmann

THE SPECTACLE AT THE TOWER

OUR CONQUEST

BALZAC'S HORSE

THE FILM EXPLAINER

LUCK

LICHTENBERG AND
THE LITTLE FLOWER GIRL

GERT HOFMANN

THE PARABLE OF
THE BLIND

Translated by Christopher Middleton

With a new afterword by Michael Hofmann

A Verba Mundi Book
David R. Godine · Publisher · Boston

This is a Verba Mundi Book
Published in 2017 by
DAVID R. GODINE, *Publisher*
Post Office Box 450
Jaffrey, New Hampshire 03452

LIBRARY OF CONGRESS CATALOGING-IN-PUBLICATION DATA
Names: Hofmann, Gert, author. |
Middleton, Christopher, 1926– translator. |
Hofmann, Michael, 1957 August 25– author of afterword.
Title: The parable of the blind / Gert Hofmann ;
translated from the German by Christopher Middleton,
with a new afterword by Michael Hofmann.
Other titles: Blindensturz. English
Description: First Verba Mundi edition. |
Jaffrey, New Hampshire : Verba Mundi,
David R. Godine, Publisher, Inc., 2016. |
Includes bibliographical references and index.
Identifiers: LCCN 2015051428 | ISBN 9781567925630 (alk. paper)
Classification: LCC PT2668.0376 B5613 2016 | DDC 833/.914—dc23
LC record available at http://lccn.loc.gov/2015051428

FIRST PRINTING
Printed in the United States of America

THE PARABLE OF THE BLIND

1

On the day when we're to be painted – yet another new day! – a knocking on the barn door drags us out of our sleep. No, the knocking isn't inside us, it's outside, where the other people are.

What's going on? we call. And it's hard to find the way back. We're in a dream. Lying in a fresh furrow, in a boundless field, half on the surface, half below ground, clouds probably overhead. One leg is stuck in the earth already, the other still outside it. Around us thick soft flakes of snow, clearly remembered, are falling into the gentle folds of the countryside and burying everything: the plow, the weeds, the trees, as well as all the other things we gave up long ago, but which probably still exist. Eventually the snow buries our second leg too, which had been lifted against the sky, like a black stone, until the last moment. Good, it's over now, we say, and we've been buried. First as far as others are concerned, then as far as we ourselves are. We're beginning to be forgotten. Back again to themselves they drag us, with their knocking. Yes, we call as we crouch there. Now what do you want of us?

Easy now, easy, the knocker says, and he's standing close to the door. And he asks if we've forgotten about being painted today.

Painted? we ask.

Yes, painted.

And why are we going to be painted?

But the knocker doesn't know.

Not forgotten, we call nevertheless, and we kick our way out of the straw we've shared all night with the mice.

Good, so we must get up now and go to the village green, it's time, the knocker says. We must refresh ourselves before being painted. Also we have to walk around in the village a bit, to practice.

This village? we ask and tap on the barn floor.

Yes, this one.

What's it called?

Pède-Sainte-Anne.

Is the sun up yet?

No.

And why not? Won't it be coming up today?

But the knocker doesn't know that, either.

And why walk around?

Because we've got to practice the walking that will be painted, the knocker says. Especially the stumbling and falling, the different kinds of fall.

But aren't we going to be painted sitting?

No, not sitting, the painter says.

So we're going to be painted walking?

Stumbling and falling and screaming.

Do we have to practice screaming?

He doesn't know. Probably we'll have to.

Wait, we call, we're coming.

Slowly, clawing at one another, we get out of the straw, struggle to our feet. Then we grope at ourselves and at one another. For there are several of us, even if only one speaks, the others listen. (Even if one speaks for all, each thinks for himself.) Then we pass our hands over our bodies. Yes, we're still the same people as yesterday. And probably to the end we'll be yesterday's people and gradually now we remember ourselves better, down to the smallest details. Everything comes back again, even what was buried, and we're very startled. We remember our names again too, the names we call one another. And this morning, as we feel our heads, arms, and sticks, we're probably the same for others. We wear thick hairy doublets festooned with grass, straw, and feathers, with long cords trailing down to our calves (recently one of us hanged himself with just such a cord), round bonnets pulled well down, and long sticks we've cut for ourselves, to pass over the ground when we walk, so that we can feel what's ahead or coming our way. What we haven't got is a nozzle or sucker, not necessarily a long one. Something with which to pull close to us, without our having to stoop, whatever might be lying before us, draw it up to our faces, so as to snuffle it, smell it. Also people could recognize us by such nozzles, even from a distance, and see what was coming. Yes, we should all have nozzles, but we haven't. Instead, we have our sticks and a begging sack thrown around our shoulders. And the horse blanket which we wrap around ourselves at night and which in the morning hangs down fore and aft, like a second skin. So we stoop and slide about on our knees and hit on a shoe, finding then the second shoe too we slip into them. And around our legs and calves we wind wrappings. Then we pull on our smocks, that's to say each of us pulls another's on for him. Bellejambe pulls Ripolus' on for him, Ripolus helps Slit Man, we pull Malente's on for him, and Malente helps us. The smocks are buttoned up at the throat, they reach to our calves. Some are badly stitched, the hems are frayed. This is how we'll be painted, it will be quite a big picture, because there are several of us, six perhaps. And we pick from one another the twigs, earth, and straw left on us from the night. We grope

9

at one another's faces, we want to clean our faces too. Doing this we feel the nose, the forehead, the eyelids, how long, how high, how broad and angled this way or that, in this or that way smashed. On top, our hoods and our bonnets. (No hat, the wind would take it away.) But we don't want to think about that now – everything in its own good time – instead we trot, sticks in hand, to the barn door. Which, with our first combined effort of the day, we push open, to break out into the village, if only with our heads at first, gasping. The morning breeze is waiting out there, it blows toward us. We stand and look in the direction where we suppose the sun should be. Yes, that's where it must be! And we rub ourselves against the doorposts right and left and stamp our feet a bit, so that our clothes will hang from us properly in folds.

Is it them? a child asks, standing just in front of us.

Yes, it's them, the knocker says.

And they really don't see me? the child asks.

That's right.

And you, the child asks, do they see you?

No, the knocker says, not me, either. And he pauses, so that the child will have time to look at us closely. But they don't need to, he says then, they've got eyes in the back of their heads, like some animals. With those they feel what's going on around them, they don't need any in front. Isn't that so? he asks, you don't need any eyes?

That's so, we say, we don't need any eyes.

And we hesitate, want to say something more, but our thoughts slip away from us.

Even then, the child says, I don't believe they're blind, and he comes closer still, breathing hard up at us. Then he asks if he can touch us.

Where? the knocker says and rustles in the leaves.

Their face.

All right, touch if you want, he says.

Then through the morning breeze the child's warm hand comes and strokes our cheeks, right and left, and creeps into our ears.

Can you feel that? the child asks.

Yes, we say, we can feel it.

And this? he asks, passing his fingertips softly over our eyelids.

Yes, that too, we say.

And how is it, the child asks, does it hurt?

No, we say, it doesn't hurt.

And if I press a bit?

No, we say, you mustn't press.

But you don't see anything anyway.

All the same, we say, you mustn't press.

Oh well, the child says, if I'm not allowed to press I won't touch, and he steps back again. No, I don't think they're blind, he says a moment later, probably after wiping his hand on his trousers. Last year there were some here too, they said they were blind as well. And then they stole three chickens and vanished again.

Yes, we've heard about that, we say, but it wasn't us, and we arrange ourselves in a low row facing the child. Those are the people who always arrive before we do and say we're them.

Since when?

Ah, we say, it started several years ago.

And why do they arrive before you and say they're you?

We don't know that, we say.

And who are they, really?

We don't know that either, we say. Anyway people tell us, wherever we go: You've been here before. But we haven't, at least we don't remember. We don't steal chickens either. We can't even see chickens.

But if you're really blind, the child asks, how can you always be looking at me when I talk?

Are we looking at you?

Well, the child says, sometimes you do look past me or over my head.

You see? we say. That's because we don't see you, little angel, we don't even look at you, we only look in the direction your voice is coming from, silly.

All the same, the child says to the knocker, they aren't all blind.

They are, every one of them, the knocker says, or else they wouldn't be going to be painted today.

One evening in the summertime when it was very hot they were sitting underneath a cherry tree and birds came. The birds sat on their shoulders and pecked their eyes out.

What sort of birds?

Crows, or ravens.

And they let them do it?

Ah, the knocker says, it all happened so fast.

Is that true? the child says and turns to face us again.

Yes, we say and nod, it's true.

And why then did they peck your eyes out?

Because we killed their young.

And why did you kill their young?

We'd had enough of their noise, we say, at least we thought we had.

Except that some people say, the knocker says, that it wasn't ravens or crows, but jackdaws.

Jackdaws, the child says, ah yes, I've heard about the thing with the jackdaws.

Yes, we say, perhaps it was jackdaws.

Well, the child says, if it was jackdaws, then I know about it. And hearing, the child asks the knocker, can they still hear?

Hear, yes, the knocker says and walks around us.

So they hear everything we're saying now?

Yes, the knocker says, that much they do hear.

And what the people in the houses say?

They hear that too, but not everything.

So they hear as much as we do?

Yes, just about.

Well, at least they're strong, the child says and takes hold of our arms.

They have to be.

Why?

Because they have to walk a lot.

And where are they going to walk to now?

Now, the knocker says, they're going to be fed, the painter has paid for it. Then they'll go to the pond, to practice falling.

Falling? the child asks, why?

Because it'll be painted, the knocker says.

And why will it be painted?

I don't know.

May I guide them to the pond? the child asks.

If you like, the knocker says. Then he claps his hands and calls: Right, now let them pass.

Cautiously, heads down, sticks right or left, bonnets pulled still farther down, we shove our way out through the barn door and enter into nature. Where at once a wind is blowing from above, from the trees, around our heads. The houses we'll be walking between are gathered already around us, quietly we ramble in among them. Windows and doors are being unbolted, people walk out and yawn, acknowledge us, utter little cries, and think: How strange that they have heads with brains inside, like other people. And they wonder if we're wise or foolish, and probably they gaze after us too as we pass.

Hey, you, we say as we walk on, are there any people here?

Yes, the child says.

How many?

Shall I count them?

No, just roughly.

Ten, perhaps.

Where? we ask.

In front of their houses.

And what do they want?

To see you.

So they're looking at us? we ask.

Yes.

Now?

Yes, now.

Well then, we say. And we huddle closer together, as we always do when we're being watched, we look more steeply upward. And feel how we're being *seen*, partly from close, partly from afar. When we lurch along their streets, we're a deep-sea monster, a general, noiseless, dark, laboriously shifted thing. Which, when displayed, is met with fear, pity, and disgust. This knot of gray bodies rolling along our street and unfolding at the windows, they think, it's them. How closely they cling to one another, how they wobble in the slight wind! And they ask themselves how such beings are possible, but that's something even we don't know. Then a church bell rings, necessarily, but it startles us.

Pity for the blind! we call and wave our sticks, so that people will get out of our way. (When they stop being afraid of our sticks, we show them our eyes.) Then we ask about the crows.

Also we ask about the season, because we're never sure of it. Certainly it's a cool day, but what does that mean in a country with so much winter? We ask: Springtime? Yes, they say, springtime. We ask: Soon? Yes, soon. Well then, we think, so it's springtime, and we try to sniff a little warmth out of the wind, and we tap our way onward, a little heartened. Perhaps it's the village green we're creeping over, perhaps we aren't there yet.

Should I guide you? the child asks, but we don't answer. We call: Pity for the blind! Yes, take them by the hand, guide them to the table with the food, the knocker says, they'll be hungry.

Are you hungry? the child asks and rustles through the leaves.

Yes, hungry, we say.

You're always hungry, the knocker says, aren't you?

Always hungry, we say. Then we say: Spare a thought for the blind, and we wave our sticks.

Then the child says we'll soon reach the table, just a few more steps. Then you can eat whatever you want, just take it. But you mustn't drop anything, because you'll never find it again.

And where's the table, we ask, and already we can smell the food. And from sheer greed we stamp our feet a bit.

There, the child says, there's the table.

And the food, we ask, where's the food?

Here, the child says and takes us by the arm.

2

After the child has led us to the table and we've placed our hands on it and have drawn our fingers around its edge and over its surface, we do then find the food, its smell floats toward us. On the table heavy bowls have been placed and fat jugs set up.

There's the food, the child says, it's all for you.

And he takes our hands and lays them on the bread and the vessels and pushes us around the table. We grope for the food, we want to know what's been provided. And our hands even go into the milk, which stands by the food, it trickles down us, lukewarm. But that's usual. We're always lunging into things we can't count on. Or else we reach out for something that doesn't exist.

Don't you sit down when you eat? the child asks.

Certainly we do, we say, is there anything to sit on?

There, the knocker says, push them onto the bench.

And why, the child asks, don't they go indoors?

No, the knocker says. They'll eat here by the door.

Sit, you may sit down, the child says and pushes us onto the bench we're to sit on. Then they put spoons into our hands for the liquids, the soft things. And so, early this morning, after they've pulled us out of our furrow and questioned us thoroughly and guided us to our table and unbuttoned our smocks and pushed our bonnets back from our faces and tied something too, a rag, across our chests, so that we won't spill anything on our doublets, we sit with our legs spread, in the cool of the season, probably around a long table by a house door on the street, and we begin to eat. We tear the bread, which is moist and still warm from the oven, we gobble into the mash.

Hey, bring us the pepper, we call and lick our fingers.

There isn't any pepper, the child says.

Then bring us salt, we say. And we scatter the salt he gives us over the bread and our hands and we feel how they're watching us.

Hey, we call, why are you staring like that?

They're not staring, the knocker says.

But we feel they're staring.

They're not staring, he says.

Ah, we say, why should we care? And we eat, first from one, then from another bowl, first cold, then hot, then lukewarm. Then a little wind comes and we're glad of our smocks. And we spoon up the mash, which is sweet, not salty, smear it into our mouths.

Look what a mess they make, they say.

Yes, we're making a mess, we say.

Then they laugh and say: Get on with it then. Get on with your sweating and stuffing yourselves.

Thanks, we say.

And so, reaching out in wider and wider circles over the table we slowly eat up every scrap and drink up every drop, first the shallower bowls, then the deep ones. The jugs, when we knock against them, sound hollower and hollower. Then we place our hands before us and they ask: Are you full now?

Yes, we say, full now.

Then they come and untie our rags and give us back our sticks. We bang on the ground with them.

You've eaten a lot, the child says.

Eaten a lot, we say.

And did you enjoy it? the child asks.

Enjoyed it, we say. Except that one of us, it's Slit Man, says the meat was hard.

Hard? the knocker asks, and he leans over us.

He means the meat was tough, we say, he's forgotten the word.

Is that true, the knocker asks him, did you mean to say tough?

Yes, Slit Man says, I meant to say tough.

He's Slit Man, we say and hold his head up. He didn't mean to complain about anything. It's just that he hasn't got any teeth left, he finds everything tough.

That's right, Slit Man says, I find everything tough. I didn't mean to complain.

Well, the knocker says, if it was tough we'll cook it longer next time, if there's a next time. Then he calls out: They've spilled things on themselves, Lise. So she comes and stoops over us and rubs at our smocks.

Yes, we say, clean us up, Lise, we're going to be painted today. Hey, we say, come closer. And we take the woman by the wrist and shoulders and pull her down to us. And now, we whisper, listen, Lise. Can you see any tobacco on the table?

No, she says, I don't see any tobacco.

Have you had a good look?

Yes, she says, I don't see any tobacco.

And are there any other tables here, where there might be some tobacco?

No, there aren't any others.

Just listen, the child exclaims, they've only just eaten all that food and now they want to smoke.

Don't shout so, we say, what we want is between you and us, not everyone need hear of it.

If it's tobacco you want, the knocker says, there isn't any, at least not for you. Perhaps the painter will give you some, if he's satisfied with you. And to the child he says: Take them away now.

To the pond?

No, behind the barn.

We wipe our hands on our trousers and bless those who fed us. In the name of the most important saints, we say and grip our sticks more tightly and are even meaning to kneel down when the child takes us by the arms and leads us away from the table.

Hey, we call, and where are you taking us?

Behind the barn, the child says, or don't you need to?

Yes, we might, we say and trot along. And we ask if the sun has risen *now*.

No, the child says, not yet.

So we still haven't got any shadows?

No, not yet.

And crows, we ask, are there crows?

Yes, there are crows.

Where?

Above us.

Can you count them? Are there five?

Yes, the child says, how do you know?

There are always five, we say. What are they doing?

They're flying.

Did you hear that, Slit Man? we ask.

Yes, Slit Man says, I heard.

And then, when we've gone a little way: Hey, we call, is it here, your barn? Here, where we're standing, or a bit farther?

A bit farther, the child says.

And we walk a bit farther and ask: So it's here? and we push our sticks into the earth, which is soft and loose hereabouts.

Yes, the child says, here.

Are there bushes?

Yes, bushes, the child says.

And are we alone now?

Yes, alone.

And then, after we've quickly kicked away a dog that had been circling us at the table and had followed us when we'd left it and is still trying to snuffle at us, and when we've unbuttoned our smocks and trousers, we call out: Hey, where are you?

Here, the child says, I'm here.

Then come closer, we say, you needn't be frightened. We want to put our hands on your head.

Why?

So we can feel you.

And why do you want to feel me?

So we'll know you're there.

As close as this? the child asks, and he comes very close.

Yes, we say, as close as that. And now tell us, little angel, we say after putting our hands on his head and pressing it a bit and imagining him for such a long time that we can almost see him, do you live here?

No, the child says and places his hand on our shoulder and tries to push us down into the damp grass.

Don't do that, we say, we have to wait a bit. First tell us where you come from.

From the forest.

Do you know your way around here?

A little.

Then listen carefully, we say. Is Pède-Sainte-Anne a big village?

No.

So it's small?

Not small either.

So it's neither big nor small?

Yes.

And what are the people like?

Same as everywhere else.

So not rich?

No.

Poor then?

Yes, more like poor.

Do they take pity on the blind?

Same as everywhere else.

Then listen, we say and let our hands rest on his hair a bit longer, who paid for our food this morning?

The painter.

He had us brought here?

I think so.

So he lives in the village?

No. In the town. But he has a house here. The one by the pond. Sometimes he comes here.

And what does he do when he comes?

He walks around and stands in front of the trees.

Which ones?

One after another.

So all of them?

Yes.

And then?

He looks at them.

Are the trees here different from other trees?

No, they're the same as everywhere else.

And then? What does the painter do then?

Then he paints.

Aha, he paints, we exclaim and pinch his cheeks.

And what does he paint, little angel?

Everything. The bridge, the church, the river, but especially the trees.

And people?

People too.

And blind people, listen, does he paint blind people? we ask and shake the child a bit, so he'll remember better. Because indeed we know that the painter wants to paint us, but we don't yet believe it. (We've never been painted before!) Isn't there anybody else for him to paint?

Yes, there is, trees.

Ah, trees, that's not much, we exclaim. We mean: people like us.

I don't know about that.

You don't know about that?

No.

Strange that he wants to paint us, we're thinking. For we know that people don't like to see us, even when we're unpainted, that's to say as we *are*. Still far off, when they see us coming, they keep out of our way, squeeze past us. We're the opposite of our friends the cripples, we don't bring good luck, they think. And if they had their way they'd gladly throw us into a deep hole they'd dug in the earth and bury us safely, so we'd be out of their way. Certainly they wouldn't paint us. Least of all want to hold on to us by painting, make us double by painting us. No, we say, a hole's better.

What?

Nothing, we say, the hole slipped out because we were just thinking about it, don't let it bother you. Instead, answer our question: Has he ever painted people like us?

No, the child says, mostly trees.

And why does he paint trees?

I don't know, the child says, so they can be seen.

Little angel, we exclaim, you're a big fool, can't they be seen in any case? Trees, we exclaim, trees, there, and there, can't you see them, and we point straight ahead and behind us, where there are probably trees that the child probably sees. Or aren't there any trees?

Yes, there are, the child says, but only little ones.

That makes no difference, we say, they can still be seen.

Yes, the child says, they can be seen.

You see? we say.

But not always, the child says and finally pulls his head away from beneath our hands. In the winter, for instance, they can't be seen, they're covered with snow.

Yes, we say, the trees perhaps, but not people.

Are people covered with snow too, perhaps?

No, but they can't always be seen, either.

Why not?

Because one day they die, the child says, then they can't be seen anymore, and that's why he paints them. And that's why he also paints himself, so that he'll always be seen.

Did he tell you so?

No, but that's what I thought.

At least you know him?

Yes.

And what does he look like? we ask.

He's tall and thin, with wild hair and paintbrushes in his hand. Sometimes I grind colors for him.

Does he talk to you?

Hardly ever.

So he's not friendly?

Yes, he is, but he doesn't talk.

And how should we know that he's friendly?

Now and then he smiles.

Stupid, we say, we can't see that. Doesn't he at least laugh sometimes?

I've never seen him laugh.

What if something's funny?

Perhaps he thinks nothing is funny.

Well, perhaps he's friendly, we say, but silly too, we say, or else he'd never have hit on the idea of painting us. A picture of us – you might as well throw it away.

Why?

Because nobody wants to see it, we say. Do you think we could ask him why he wants to paint us?

You can always ask.

Then tell us when we should ask.

Yes, I'll tell you.

And the sun, we ask, after we've stood around for a bit longer and digested our food and thought about things, is it there now?

No.

Then show us at least where it rises, just in case it does, we say.

And the child takes hold of our smocks and turns us around and says: That's where it'll rise, there, and he pushes us to face in the direction of the sun. And we hearken in that direction for a while and say: Good, we'll remember it. And now, angel, look the other way a bit, so we'll be alone a bit, when we're relieving ourselves, we say and push the child aside and let our trousers down. But when we're crouching in the cold and tickly grass we sense that we're not alone at all, there's a breathing and gasping and giggling in front of us and behind us. They're all still there! Probably they followed us from the table and are standing around us now.

Hey! we call, who's there and what do you want?

But they only giggle. Go away, whoever's there, we call and, still crouching, strike out around us with our sticks but only hit one another. Animals! we call.

Then somebody says: Animals yourselves.

Who said that?

I did.

We aren't asking who it was, we say, you should be ashamed of saying that, whoever you are.

You should be ashamed too.

Beast, we exclaim.

Ah, the knocker says, don't shout so loud. And you there, leave them in peace.

Peace, we exclaim, what's that? We're punished, we say, till the end of our days, but soon we'll have passed on. Yet we're still alive and we still have our dignity, while other people are human only in form but in all other ways they're beasts. For we are the Lord's elect, because He punishes those whom He loves, amen. (Even if His Love goes a bit too far, sometimes, we're thinking.) Then a girl or a young woman, perhaps in a cow shed or a yard, suddenly starts to sing. Her song comes to us across a few roofs, or so we imagine. We sob a bit and hum along with her a bit, then the girl stops and everything goes quiet again. And then, shoulder to shoulder and with our thighs apart, probably behind the barn, hands clenched on our knees, after we've relieved ourselves side by side before them and the men and women of the village of Pède-Sainte-Anne have seen their fill of us and giggled their fill, well, then we're ready and we want to leave this place just as quickly as we can.

Hey, we call, we want to leave this place, we want to forget about all this right away. We've still got to practice falling, so we have to cross the village green. Hey, we call, where's the village green? Can somebody guide us?

You're on the village green, somebody says.

Oh, we say and cover our nakedness and pull up our trousers, aren't we behind the barn?

Yes, he says, you're behind the barn.

Are we? we ask, so is the barn on the village green?

Yes, on the village green, he says and laughs. Then somebody kicks us in the calf, but it doesn't hurt much.

Hey, we exclaim, why are you kicking us?

And the knocker says: Yes, why did you kick them?

I didn't kick them, the child says – the one who'd wanted to guide us to the pond.

But somebody did, we say, we felt it.

He did kick them, another child says, I saw.

And why did he kick them? the knocker asks.

Ah, says the child who wanted to guide us to the pond, just because.

Well, we say, just so long as he doesn't kick us again, this time it didn't hurt. Will you promise not to kick us again?

I don't know yet, the child says.

Won't you take them to the pond now? the knocker asks.

No, the child says, I don't like them.

No matter, we'll find the pond, even without you, we say and step back, because it's our duty to step back so we won't get in anybody's way. And so we've emptied ourselves on the village green, not behind the barn, but this doesn't surprise us. We're always too quick to believe people when they say we're

27

somewhere. When they say: You're in a church, we feel: A church, yes indeed, even if it's only a mill, or, let's say, a tavern. And when they say: You're on a hill, we feel: Ah, a hill. Even when, surrounded by a lot of flat country, we're in a hollow. This isn't important, though. The fact is that anywhere we are is where we are. All right, we say, we're leaving now.

Fine, the knocker says, off you go then.

And which way should we go? we ask.

Just go straight ahead, he says.

All right, we say, straight ahead.

And we go with God, to the pond.

3

We're always hearing it said that anyone who walks in front ought to be able to tell light from dark. Even if he doesn't see every little detail, for instance his shadow, he must be able to recognize blatant things, for instance the sunlight. Not, like us, from warmth on the skin, but as light in the eyes. Even if he can't really see, he must *almost* be able to see. This is what Ripolus is for us, Ripolus with the longest stick.

Hey, we call, Ripolus.

Yes, Ripolus says, who's that calling me?

We're calling you, we say, it's us.

And where are you, Ripolus asks and gropes for us with his stick.

We're here, we call, here.

And what do you want? Ripolus asks.

Nothing, we say, we don't want anything.

Then why are you calling me?

Because we want to hear you.

Why?

So we'll know you're still there.

And where else might I be? Ripolus asks.

Well, we call, you might ...

No, Ripolus calls, and he stamps his feet on the ground, I'm still here.

Yes, we say, we can hear you. And we line up against a fence or lattice, for we'll be walking in single file so we won't take up so much room on the way, in nature. Right, and we take hold of one another, probably by the shoulder or by the stick of whoever's walking in front of us. Or we take him by the hand, so as not to lose him. And then, after we've turned our backs on the morning sounds of the village, we walk on behind Ripolus, who probably has the same name as his father. If he does have a second name we don't know it.

Perhaps he doesn't know it anymore himself, or won't reveal it. Isn't that so? we ask.

Yes? Ripolus says, what's that?

We're wondering, we say, what your name is.

Ripolus.

Ripolus or Ripolust? we ask.

Yes, Ripolus says.

And what else, we ask, what else are you called?

Nothing else, Ripolus says.

Well, we say, that'll have to be enough. Well, we ask, have you got your stick?

Yes, Ripolus says, my stick's here. And he taps his stick over the ground, for us to be able to hear it.

Good, we say, and now stretch it out, so you'll know where you're going. So we'll know where we're treading when we walk behind you. Stretch it out, Ripolus, stretch it out, we call.

Yes, Ripolus says, I'm stretching it out now. And where are we going? he asks after we've walked a little way. For God's earth, which is infinite for everyone, is even bigger than that for us. All the same, we're making some headway, it's just a question of where to. Because we certainly don't always walk straight ahead, sometimes it's back and forth and not only forward, but back too, or in a circle. This soon prolongs, more than infinitely, the tiniest village, we'll be clinging to one another for support, one of us will be leaning on his stick and having to take deep breaths before he can go on. When that happens, a crutch mightn't be a bad thing. Helped by it we'd fly over the earth, horizontal, with our heads drawn in. But that would mean we were cripples, not just a bit blind, the way we are. So let's be satisfied with what we have, let's creep onward supported by sticks! Or we'll wave the sticks at whatever stands in our way, people, their cattle, their dogs. True, we haven't yet collided with any, the way to the pond seems to be clear, yet if we walk a bit farther they'll certainly come. (People, who speak to us, touch us, are sorry for us, give us food and drink, and, since we can take a joke, shove us into ditches or spit into our eyes.) Yet there are birds, not only crows, close to us and they draw us onward, and they're flying, probably in smallish flocks, probably to the right, above our heads. To the left, in any case, a cow shed, whence a stamping comes. Also we can smell the cow shed smells, they come out through the cracks. One of us, we forget who, can even *feel* the cow shed, he comes from the country.

There's a cow shed, he says, and there's another cow shed. And here comes another.

And how do you know that? we ask.

Because I can feel cow sheds.

And what do you feel them with? we ask.

But he doesn't know that either. Also he can't feel all cow sheds, even if he can feel some.

And ponds, we ask, can you feel ponds?

No, he doesn't feel ponds.

And why don't you feel ponds?

I simply don't, he says, and on we trot.

Hey, Ripolus, we call, did you hear that, he can't feel the pond. Hey, Ripolus, when will the pond be coming?

Any moment, Ripolus says, the pond will be there any moment.

And what's stopping us, we ask.

It's the distance, Ripolus says.

We walk and walk, we say, and aren't and aren't there yet.

Any moment, Ripolus says, any moment.

And when's that, when's any moment? we ask because we're in a hurry to get to be painted at last. And Ripolus doesn't know *when* that will be, either. And what's it *like*, we ask, to be painted?

What'll it be like? Ripolus says, it'll be fine.

Fine like pissing? we ask.

No, Ripolus says, much finer.

You see, that's why we're in a hurry, we say. And we're trotting through a region which is probably one of the more beautiful, or anyway less ugly, on earth, so they say. A region where brown and green melt quietly into one another and the ground is soft and fat and moist and level. And the flatness of the fields is relieved by trees, crooked or straight, which look as if they'd been dabbed into it. So beautiful it looks almost artificial, they exclaim. And they tug excitedly at our smocks and pant into our faces. And what's so beautiful about it? we ask. Everything, they say and stamp their feet for joy, as if they were going to dance at any moment. Yes, we say, we can smell all that, but we'd rather talk about something else. And so the subject is quickly changed. And Ripolus now, with the sky of the region, which we seldom mention, probably high above his head, suddenly stops, because instead of leading us to the pond, he doesn't himself know where he's leading us.

Hey, Ripolus, we call, what's the meaning of this?

I'm stopping again, he says.

And why, we ask, are you stopping again? Do we have a shadow? Is there light overhead at last? Can we be painted now?

Perhaps.

How light, Ripolus, how light? Quick, we call, don't just stand there, describe our shadows for us. But Ripolus can't describe them for us, because instead of long and big and broad shadows, if any, we've only got short and thin ones, which he can't see.

And why did you stop then, if you haven't seen anything? we ask, are you tired again already?

But Ripolus doesn't tell us, he only trudges around us in silence. For, while he's still able to speak, he only speaks a little, perhaps even less than we do. Since he has only a dim picture of what exists in front of us, around us, and behind us – it was always much and apparently there's more and more of it – he forgets the words for it, just like we do. (Also for what's inside him, or was, or could be inside him, those words too he forgets, as we do, exactly as we do.) Many of the words he once knew, the *words from before*, as he calls them, he's already forgotten, at least half of them, no wonder his sentences (and ours) are getting shorter and shorter. Compared with the sentences from before they aren't even sentences. But none of this disturbs him, because he believes that when all the words have been forgotten, then there'll be nothing above, beneath, before, or inside us. And if he does (or we do) still remember an old sort of word, or if somebody speaks such a word, he doesn't know if the thing is still behind the word and how he's to think about it. A larch tree clearing? Good, but how? A twilight? Fine, but what's that? And he wonders where it belongs, what are the connections? Then there always has to be somebody who'll explain it for him (or us). Other words that he hears don't remind him (us) of anything anymore, all he can do is shrug. Possibly there used to be some such thing a long time ago. Or a word means to remind us of something, but of what, of what? We stop in our tracks, or, if we happen to be lying down, we sit up, and we pull close to us with clammy hands the expression from before, hold it, in a manner of speaking – everything is in a manner of speaking – close to our eyes or nose or mouth. And we snuffle at it, smell it, and lick it, gently, gently, gently. Is it possible that we once really understood this expression or this word, carried it around inside us? Unthinkable! We don't even know anymore how many words we've forgotten, we've forgotten even that. Even if the world slipped away from us entirely, we wouldn't miss it. Instead of pressing forward into it with words, we curl up without words inside what's still there. And, to punish ourselves for doing so, we often hit ourselves in the face, often bite our fingers. Even Ripolus does, walking in front and still feeling the light. Possibly he's not only duller and tireder than us, but older too. Yes, he's older, we think, he *must* be older. And then again: No, he's not. Perhaps he only walks and breathes as if he were older, perhaps he wants to deceive us. Admittedly, he's got no more teeth in his head, we felt that when we shoved a carrot into his mouth once and went too far with it. Yes, those were his gums, but there wasn't anything else in Ripolus' mouth. Yet even if he hasn't got any teeth left, that still doesn't prove much. Lots of people have no teeth and still aren't older than we are. Anyway, walking uphill Ripolus starts to gasp, sweats when he's arrived at the top, has to stop for long spells to catch his breath, and likes to lean against trees, particularly birches and lime trees. And he exclaims that he's forty already, but can he prove it? Hardly, because he then says he doesn't think of his age and has forgotten it, just as we've forgotten ours. Now he's leading us in the direction of the sun, that's to say, in the direction he thinks is the brightest.

Hey, Ripolus, we call.

Yes, he says, I'm here.

All right, Ripolus, what can you see? Simply describe for us what you see.

Oh, Ripolus says, not much.

Why, we ask, because not much is there or because you can't see it?

I can't see it, he says, I can't see anything, but probably there's not much to be seen, either. This region, just as I thought, he says and taps his foot on it, is not heavily populated.

But there's a village, isn't there? we ask.

Yes, he says, a small one.

And people, we ask, can you see people?

People, he asks, and probably he's looking around.

No, he says.

Can't you see any, we ask, or is that only what you think?

It's what I think, he says.

Right, we say, but *what can you see*, really?

What I can really see?

Yes.

I see, Ripolus says, and probably he makes a sweep, probably with his right hand. Also in describing what he sees he makes something of a wide sweep. He sees a plain, something flat, at least that's what it all comes down to. Yes, it'll be a plain I'm seeing, he says, a plain that we're facing, no, beneath us. Then he pauses again.

So it's a plain? we ask.

Yes.

But, we bellow, it isn't a plain we're looking for, you fool, you shouldn't be seeing a plain!

Shouldn't I?

No.

All right, he says. Then perhaps I'm not seeing one. I'm probably seeing...

Yes?

What should I be seeing? he asks.

A pond, we exclaim.

A pond?

Yes, a pond.

No, Ripolus says, after probably gazing for a while over the plain before us, which he perhaps sees, but also perhaps only imagines. I don't see any pond. But of course it might be covered up.

What by?

By trees, for instance.

And the trees, we ask, can you see them?

No, Ripolus says, I can't see them. I'm not seeing much at all today. I can't even see the sky.

What, we exclaim, can't you even see the sky?

No, Ripolus says, probably I can't.

So you're not sure?

Not altogether.

Then don't just stand there, we exclaim, move about, move about, at least inside your head. It could just be that something's there and you'll end up seeing it. Ripolus, we exclaim, you've got to find the pond, take a really good look around. It must be very close, we can almost smell it. And we give him a little time too, so that he can look around, and we turn as he turns and ask him if there's anything there.

No.

And over there?

No, nothing there either.

And this way, we ask, do you see anything this way?

But Ripolus, because he's having a bad day, simply doesn't see the pond even that way. Either there isn't one, he says, or we've lost our way.

Curse it, we say.

Yes, he says, we've lost our way. So what do we do now? he asks.

You'll have to turn back.

And where, Ripolus asks, will you be going?

We'll follow you, we say, we'll follow you.

And where, Ripolus asks, will I be going?

To the house with the painter.

Right, Ripolus says, so we'll turn back.

4

Then, as we carry on walking, in another direction, there's Slit Man coming up behind Ripolus. Unfortunately he's a thief. We forget his name while we're walking, it comes back to us at night. So that we'll be able to imagine Slit Man to ourselves, Ripolus has often described him to us. He tells us that he's small and nimble, with thick wrists and thick knees on which he rests his hands while he sits down. And we believe him. In fact, we believe everything Ripolus tells us about the look of things, their *exterior*, whenever we want to have a picture of what's in front of us and behind us. Anyway Slit Man lost his eyesight not in the natural way like us, but in the other way, the human way.

I had amazing eyes, he often says, and I'd still have them today, if . . .

Then he likes to weep. The eyes were supposedly blue, at least that's what he says. And, as people kept assuring him in those days, they always took on a green tint near the sea, but also near fairly large lakes and rivers. At night, like cat's eyes, they shone. With eyes like those, Slit Man says, one can see everything.

Well, we say, a lot perhaps, but – everything?

Yes, he exclaims, everything.

Well, we say, a lot perhaps, but surely not . . .

Anyway everything one wants to see, Slit Man says, everything that interests one, even if one didn't remember the
details. Even on darkish nights he could discern every star,
and in the grass every butterfly.

And the worms, we ask, did you see the worms too?

Yes, he says, the worms too.

Well, we listen to this, but should we believe him? Perhaps
he did have eyes like that, perhaps he didn't. Perhaps he only
imagined them, when it was all over, when he no longer had
any. It's said that in the village of Peer, just as he was stealing
the foot bone of Saint William from the church, he was caught
with the relic in his hand and only by a hair's breadth escaped
being hanged. Now to enter eternity with a rope around your
neck is terrible, of course. So, on account of a plea made by
the canon of the church, who has guests sitting around his
oak table with him at the time, to the regret of everyone in the
neighborhood Slit Man isn't to be hanged but only slit. How
Slit Man screams for mercy, as soon as he hears this! All right
then, the slitting is postponed. How he breathes again! Just so
that for one more day he can consider and absorb the edifice
of the world, which in its incomprehensible beauty the Lord
established, after all, for him too. Good, and now comes the day
set aside for him and his eyes. Over his face he has smeared dirt
and ashes, to let everybody know he's penitent. He stands at the
window of his small prison, where, despite the dull weather,
huge masses of light assault him. His hands rest on the window
bars, his gaze rests on the square outside, where he sees the
people going past, but only up to their calves. Every so often
somebody stoops and looks in on him. Eyes and mouth agape,
he considers the world now as he never did before, and he
discerns it and absorbs it. Even if not as a whole – nobody can
do that – still some parts of it: by day the clouds, by night the

stars, and at all times the random but inexhaustible patterns on the wall of his small prison and the small animals creeping on him, which he crushes to death with his thumb. He's so greedy that he even starts to *count* the little hairs on his right hand. All this he absorbs, but he feels it won't be enough (for the rest of his life, what's left of it). On the day before he got slit, the door had opened, creaking, and he'd been shown the instruments, so that he'd be able to include them in his picture of the world. These are, in a flat leather case, two knives, which the executioner has hastily brought from Brussels and now places ceremoniously in front of him. For they are part of the world which had not been apparent before and which must now be quickly *absorbed*, along with everything else: two butcher's knives, with handles of bone, blades thin but long and broad. The longer of the two is already a bit rusted near the handle, that's just part of its peculiarity. Both, when he holds them in the light, look notched and old-fashioned, and they seem to have been put to various uses, as well as frequently sharpened. After the future Slit Man has wrestled for a long time with Satan, shoulder against shoulder, staring at the knives, the executioner takes them away from him, having now tied a long leather apron around his own waist. It is Sunday, the people of the neighborhood must be given time to arrive. But birds too, mostly ravens and crows, come and sit around hungrily in the trees and on the rim of the well in the marketplace. And here, after evening Mass, when everyone is gathered in fine weather and with a good view right up into the sloping streets, he becomes famous, if only for a little while, at least people are talking about him a lot. After this, as if a signal had been given, the hush of the crowd, he alone screams. Up till the last moment he'd believed that what's now happening can't happen, because he can't imagine it, that it's only a threat,

41

the lords and masters having only wanted to give him a fright. Now he discovers he was wrong. Ever since that evening the crows, which in his hour of trouble sat before him on the rim of the well, with him, have been his traveling companions, so he believes. He can clearly remember four, but more arrive. Mornings they flutter around him, travel above him from tree to tree. Toward nightfall they descend around him, sit at his feet and try to perch on his shoulders, but he chases them away.

Get away, what more do you want of me, he calls, and he's convinced that on that day in May they ate up his eyes.

It's you they're after, we say, you.

Can anyone here see them? he asks.

Not us, we say, not us. And you, Ripolus, can you see them? No, Ripolus says, not quite.

Curse it, Slit Man says, and how many are there?

Probably five, Ripolus says.

Curse it, Slit Man calls, more and more of them.

They want you, we say, and we laugh.

Whether or not their number increases we don't know, perhaps yes, perhaps also no. We don't know where they are at night, either, in the trees, we believe. Or on a barn roof, it occurs to us, if one's nearby. And we hearken, but can't hear any roof or trees. Or they fly into the nearest forest, to break out of it again in the morning and wait for us, when we push our way out of our barn. Even now, quite a while after being slit, Slit Man can't understand them. He'll finally see the true light, you'd think, but he doesn't. Instead, he deludes himself into thinking it's all only a dream. And that he only has to raise his eyelids and the world will be there again. (Yet he has no eyelids to raise now.) And he sleeps, if at all, briefly, burrowed deep into the straw, when he thinks it's nighttime, and moans and wails when he lies down, but also when he gets up again.

Yes, even in his sleep he moans. There's never a morning comes but he looks up and wants to see the sun.

The sun, he exclaims, I don't see the sun, when we commonly suppose it's somewhere in the sky.

That doesn't matter, we say, we don't see it either.

I don't care if you see it, he exclaims, *I* should be the one who's seeing it.

Quiet now, we say, it's all over and done with, but he can't keep quiet.

I sat there, he says, they'd tied me up . . .

Don't think about it anymore, we say.

They'd tied me up and . . .

Come on now, we say, let's take a walk.

And we take him among us and hold him by the arms and haul him along with us a little way, perhaps underneath some trees. So that he'll have different thoughts and be moving around a bit. An ugly person, who, when we pass our fingers over his forehead, has no eyebrows left, probably not even ears. They slit everything off him. We're also surprised when we feel his bonnet, which is made for a much bigger head, it hangs down over him. With the head he's got, how can he wear a bonnet like that? Well, it's the only bonnet he's got. He's even plucked his hair out. All the same, he'll be painted together with us.

But he's not one of us.

Yes he is, they tell us, now he is.

But he hasn't got any ears.

That makes no difference.

And if he's a thief?

That doesn't matter.

All right then, we say. And we're thinking: Yes, it'd be foolish not to say good-bye to him soon. And at the right moment not to push him into a ditch, or, while he's having a drink, into a stream. Except that moment hasn't arrived yet, but it will, it will. Hey, Slit Man, we call and spit between our feet, you know something?

No, he says, what?

You're going to be painted.

I know.

And why are you going to be painted?

I don't know.

Nor do we, we say. Do you steal things still?

Why, he asks, are you missing something?

Not yet, we say, not yet.

Yes, we know a lot about him, more than he thinks, and God knows even more. Sometimes from the floor of a barn he'll take a piece of wood or a smooth stone and hide it on his person, in the most unbelievable places. A habit, we think. Under other circumstances, if the light were better, of course he'd have taken something else from the barn floor, or from the kitchen, but he can't find things anymore now. Isn't that so, we ask, you don't steal anymore?

It's difficult, Slit Man says.

Why, we ask, isn't there anything left to steal?

Certainly there is, Slit Man says, only I can't see it.

And he's restless, takes wheat kernels from the pockets of his smock and munches them and hangs his mouth in every stream we hear murmuring. And walks only if we push him forward, always stooping low over the ground. And if he goes on creeping like that he'll surely be a hunchback soon. And he croaks and drools and froths at the mouth and if we're not careful he'll pass his restlessness on to us, then we'll froth and croak too, but we don't let things go that far.

Quiet now, quiet now, we say when he's all set to start frothing, and we leap on him and grab him and throw him to the

44

ground and sit on him. Or we take him by the arms and legs and drag him to the nearest tree. And even if he struggles, we tie him to the tree trunk with our cords, until his throat and shoulders slacken and slowly he quiets down. This is on our way to the pond, so we hope, still in the village, or on the edge of it, and everything is probably bare and empty, the path, the sky, the countryside. Later we walk, probably, out of the village called Pède-Sainte-Anne – or so they told us. Unless it's already behind us and we're in the next village already. In any case, a village with its church, around the tower of which birds are flying, birds we can hear squawking.

Are they mine? Slit Man asks.

Yes.

How can you know?

We recognize them.

What by?

The way they screech.

Get away, if you're mine, Slit Man shouts, and he's thinking of his eyes and he starts to froth at the mouth again. And we pull him to the nearest tree and tie him up and let him froth and then ask him: Right, are you quiet again now?

Quiet, Slit Man says.

So quiet you can be painted? we ask.

Yes, quiet as that.

But we don't believe him. His throat full of screams, his mouth full of curses! Well, he can go along with us a little, but not much longer. We'll wait until we've been painted and then we'll leave him behind. Or else we'll sit on him and try to suffocate him, then we'll be rid of him. One thing's for sure: We won't be sorry for him, he's not one of us. If he's walking with us at all, he's walking in the place that doesn't belong to him at all but to one of us who doesn't walk anymore and now lies at rest. His name was Lamme and recently he was farting along with us. Before a meal he felt sick, he lay down, turned over, and after the meal, he died. Yes, our friend Lamme is dead, we won't be seeing him again, because he had to be buried. At all events, his smock, doublet, and boots were suddenly available and belonged to us. We tossed them into a heap and crouched around them, and touched them and listened to them and sniffed at them and shared them out among us. Slit Man got most of them, because he didn't have anything and shouted loudest. Because in despair at being slit he'd torn his clothes from his body and in doing so had quite forgotten he'd need his clothes. So it turns out that he's now wearing the doublet that doesn't belong to him. Or trousers that don't belong to him. And if he's got tobacco he stuffs it into a pipe that doesn't belong to him, but which Lamme used to puff not long ago. Also his bonnet doesn't belong to him and it looks ridiculous on him. How often people who can still see laugh at this bonnet! All the same, he'll be painted with us, we don't know if it'll be in front of us or behind us. Even the stick he waves around him, which will probably be painted too, he stole even that. Well, we say and chuckle a bit, he won't be going along with us much longer. All the same, it's said he looks very like the person whose place he's walking in now. Does he think like him too?

No, he exclaims, I think differently.

And feel, we ask, do you feel as he did?

No, he feels differently too.

Fine, we say, but how, but how?

But he doesn't know that, either.

You see, we say, you're not different at all, you only think you are.

No, he says, I'm different. And then, after thinking a bit, he says that, for example, he doesn't hear well anymore, the sounds are getting fainter.

Then can't you even hear us? we ask.

Yes, I can still hear you, he says. What are you getting at?

Nothing, we say, we aren't getting at anything.

So let's be moving along now, Ripolus says.

5

So we turn back again meaning to find the house by the pond
and the painter who wants to paint us. Ripolus supposes he's
turning back again, he's not certain. Walking behind Ripolus,
we aren't certain either. Sometimes we think we're turning
back, sometimes we think we're walking onward. Who'd have
thought it was such a long way? All the same, we did dress
up warm. In doing so (dressing up) we thought as much of
ourselves as of our painting. For if somebody wants to paint
us, then he must paint us with everything we have: the smocks
with the frayed hems, the bonnets, the sticks, the legs wrapped
up and lifted, the faces turning up to the sky, as we're always
being told, with a slightly transfigured look. Perhaps too it'll
start to rain, then the day will be particularly long. True, they
say springtime is coming, but there's rain and snow in the air.
So we keep our feet warm too, that's why they're wrapped.
Also in wrappings one falls more softly, if one must needs fall.
Besides this, there's not much to paint, if we're to be painted. Of
course, there are pockets in our smocks, with various things in
them, but since the things can't be seen they can't be painted.
(Also what's in our heads, for the same reason that can't be
painted either.) Only our sticks and our bodies in our smocks
are left, and today they weigh (the bodies) particularly heavily
on the crust, the earth crust. And are walking, one behind the

other, probably down a sunken lane or a narrow alley, at the end of which, as we find out with our sticks, there's a fence blocking our path. So weren't we going straight ahead after all? No, it seems we weren't. Seemingly we've gone in the wrong direction, unless from the very start we were sent in the wrong direction. The only thing left for us to do is lean against the fence and, with eyes closed, regret we're here. Better still we could have lain down and fallen asleep. But we must press on, on, for we're going to be painted. And so we creep along the fence and call: Hey, here's a fence! Hey, we call, isn't there anybody here to tell us what this fence is doing here? And we pull our way, lath by lath, along the fence, until it stops and we're standing in a corner. Hey, we call and cling to the laths, hey, Ripolus, where are you?

I'm here, Ripolus calls, and he's standing right in our midst.

And where have you taken us?

To a fence, he says.

Yes, to a fence, we've noticed that, we call and shake the fence, but where do we go from here?

Can you see where we go from here?

No.

And the fence, we ask, can you see the fence?

No, Ripolus says, I can't see it.

And anything else, we ask, can you see anything else?

As a matter of fact, Ripolus says, I can't see anything at all.

Why not? we exclaim. And isn't there anybody else who can see the fence? And who could tell us perhaps how we get to the pond? Hey, we call, is anybody there?

Yes, a voice says, me.

Aha, we say, so there is somebody. And we'd been thinking . . .

No, the voice says, I'm here.

Good, then come closer, if you're here, we say.

Like this?

No, closer still, much closer, so we can put a hand on your head, we say.

Why?

So we'll know who you are.

Like this then?

Yes, like that, we say once he's come closer, and we put a hand on his head. True, we don't yet know who he is, but at least his head helps us to *imagine* something, even if each of us imagines something different. And now, we say, after each of us has imagined him in his own way, tell us: Where have you been all the time?

Here, he says, I was here.

Didn't you hear us calling?

Yes, I did.

Then why didn't you come and help us?

Because I don't meddle with other people's concerns.

But we'd lost our way, we've been walking in a circle.

Anyone can do what he wants.

But we hadn't wanted to walk in a circle.

How do you expect me to know that?

You could have thought it, we say. But it's all right, if you didn't know. And who are you?

Ah, the voice says, I'm just Balthasar.

No matter, Balthasar, we say. Just stay as you are and tell us: Are we still in the village?

Yes, Balthasar says, this is where it ends.

Where the church is?

No, Balthasar says, the other end.

And crows, we ask, are there crows here?

Yes, he says, there are crows here.

How many?

Six or seven.

Yes, we're thinking, that's them. They're flying around the tower here, aren't they? we ask.

No, Balthasar says, those are other ones.

Which?

Starlings.

Aha, we say, starlings fly around the tower?

No.

Where then?

Around the lime tree.

And where's that?

On the village green.

So are we still on the village green?

Yes.

And where's the pond?

Which one? There are many of them.

Not only the one where the painter lives?

Oh no.

Did you hear that, Ripolus, we say and turn probably to Ripolus, there are many ponds here and you couldn't find a single one.

Ah, Ripolus says, I'd find it if only I could see better today.

Yes, Ripolus isn't seeing anything today, we say and laugh and turn probably back to Balthasar.

And ask: And where's the pond where the painter lives?

That's one of them, Balthasar says.

So we're close to it? we ask.

Yes, close, says Balthasar. And explains to us in his quiet voice that we've gone the wrong way. We should have gone to the right, to the right! But can we, stricken as we are, talk of right and left at all? That would presuppose we know what's straight ahead, but do we really know that? But Balthasar should be telling this not to us but to Ripolus, who of course doesn't listen. No, Ripolus, like an old ram, walks to the left, and us behind him. To the right, Ripolus, you must walk to the right. Hey, we call, are you still there?

Yes, Ripolus says, I'm still here.

And you, Balthasar, are you still here?

I'm here, Balthasar says.

And where, we ask, is the fence?

That's here too, Balthasar says.

And can you see it?

Yes.

And where does it end?

There, Balthasar says, I'll show you. And he takes us by the hands and pulls us along with him and takes us to another place where there's probably no fence, we can feel there isn't. There, he says, that's where it ends.

Aha, we say, so that's it. And now the pond where the painter lives, now we want to go to the pond.

Do you know the painter?

The one who paints the trees?

Yes, we say, but he'll paint us too.

Has he said so?

No, we say, he can't, because he doesn't know us.

Then he won't paint you.

Won't he? we ask, how do you know? Are you the person who grinds his colors?

No, Balthasar says, I'm somebody else.

But you could have been?

No, he says, it's quite impossible. And he thinks for a while and then says: Yes, it might be possible.

You see? we say. Anyway, you do know the painter, do you?

Yes.

Did he ask about us?

Not me.

So you haven't seen him yet today?

No.

And have you met anybody who asked about us?

No.

And anybody who hasn't asked about us?

Not that either.

Then we walk on a bit.

And you, Balthasar asks later, who are you?

Ah, we're the people with the crows, we say. Not the people who go ahead of us, so don't get us mixed up. We can't be the people who go ahead of us, because we can't see chickens. And since he doesn't understand and hasn't yet heard of us, we tell him how, one summer night, we were sitting and talking beneath a tree and crows suddenly came and pecked out our eyes.

What sort of a tree?

A cherry tree.

And what were you talking about?

We've forgotten, we say. But it was a great misfortune and there was a lot of talk about it at the time. Haven't you ever heard of it?

No.

So perhaps you don't believe it?

No, I don't believe it.

Well, we say, whether or not you believe it is your concern, at least we've told you, so you won't be able to say you've never even heard of it.

All right, he says, I've heard it. And he thinks, when he sees that we really are all stricken in the same way and form a group, one walking so close behind the other, all keeping step, even if we aren't sure where we're going, that we're related. A numerous but united and like-minded family, hurrying on our way to the pond.

Well, we say, that's so. We may look like a family, but we aren't. One day we came out of a forest, one after the other, and since none of us had any definite plans, we walked on together, that's all. Since then, people think we belong together.

So you're not fathers and sons?

No.

And brothers, he asks, aren't you even brothers?

No, we say, we aren't brothers either. And then we stop walking and say: Hey, Slit Man, and we seek him out quickly and feel him and know him by the ears that are missing and push him toward Balthasar and say that *he*, for example, isn't one of us, he's only going along with us, taking somebody else's place.

And since when have you been going along together?

Since recently.

And how long will you stay together?

Not much longer.

And how many of you are there? Balthasar asks – he wants to test us.

We don't know exactly, we say.

And how many were you before, he asks, or don't you know that either?

Seven, we say, we were seven before, but we lost one in the noontime.

And what happened to him?

We don't know.

And the sticks, he asks, why do you have the sticks?

Because we haven't got nozzles.

So you can't even see the earth?

No, we smell it.

And the sky? Balthasar asks after walking for a while with us across a stubble field, do you smell it too?

No, we say, we hear it. And then we call: Hey, are you taking us the right way?

Yes, Balthasar says, straight ahead.

And where's that, straight ahead? Don't forget we're going to be painted any moment.

Ah, Balthasar says, but not right now.

And why not? we ask because we want to have it over and done with as soon as possible.

Because it's still too dark.

And when will it be light?

Later, Balthasar says. And now, he says after we've walked a bit farther and fallen down and gotten up again and walked on, I'll tell you something.

Over yonder, where the path leaves the village, a pig is going to be slaughtered anytime now. I've seen the butcher with his knife already sharpened.

So you mustn't be startled when you hear it squeal.

If you like, we can go and look.

Ah, we say, we wouldn't see it anyhow.

But I could describe it for you.

No, we say, it's not the same. Besides, we've got to hurry, we're going to be painted very soon.

Well, Balthasar says, then we won't go. We can hear it squeal just as well, I needn't describe that for you.

No, we say, we'll hear it.

And then we walk a bit farther and imagine the pig so precisely that we can even hear how, not far from us, it's still alive and grunting and snuffling the earth. We can even smell the fire with the caldron on it, into which the pig will be chopped up.

(But it could be another fire we're perhaps smelling.) And we hearken and wonder at every step why it doesn't finally squeal.

Was that it? we ask.

No, that wasn't it.

And that? we ask later.

No, not that either.

So nothing has squealed yet?

No, he says, not yet.

Yes, we say, just as we thought, we didn't hear anything. We only thought we should have heard something, time's getting on. And on we walk again. And ask: Hey, Balthasar, why doesn't anything squeal? But he doesn't know.

Yet it will, he says. And you, he asks later, do you see one another?

No, we say, we don't see one another either. And we think about it and then say that we feel one another.

What with, Balthasar asks, with your hands?

No, we say, we don't know what with: We feel it must be us when we say *us*. Even if we can't prove it.

And who are you?

The people in the middle.

Very well then, Balthasar says, you walk straight ahead now. I've got to be getting along to my work now.

And us, where are we going?

Straight ahead.

But we've been going straight ahead all the time.

No matter.

Are we still in the village?

Yes, he says, but not much longer.

And what comes then?

The end of the village.

The one by the church?

No, he says, the other. And then comes the pond.

Listen, we say, you must tell all that to Ripolus.

But he'll have none of it. No, he says, I'm having my bad day, I can't see anything at all. Then he stops, nevertheless, and asks: So where must I go?

Then naturally we have to stop. Balthasar probably stops too. Unless he simply walks on and leaves us.

Hey, Ripolus, we call, why are you stopping? Why aren't you walking on? Hey, Balthasar, we call, where are you? The pond, Balthasar says – already he's some way off – comes later, just walk straight ahead. Or can't you anymore?

Yes, we say, we can, but Ripolus can't. He's got warts on his feet. Quick, Ripolus, show him.

And then, while Ripolus is probably taking off his shoes to look for his warts, we ask Balthasar if he's got a toad on him, by any chance, with which to rub the warts, so Ripolus will be able to walk better, but Balthasar, who's far away already, hasn't got a toad, it's still too cold for toads.

Well, he'll just have to wait, until it gets warmer and we can find one, we say. Isn't that so, we say, you'll wait?

Yes, Ripolus says, I'll wait.

Hey, we call later after we've waited a while and Ripolus has put his shoes back on, is anybody here besides us? Hey, Ripolus, can you see anybody?

But Ripolus can't see anybody either. No, he says, unfortunately I can't.

And then, since we're not certain whether Balthasar is still with us, we call: Hey, Balthasar, are you still here? But Balthasar doesn't answer, so we must be alone. Even then – always this feeling that somebody is seeing us, from above, at an angle, somebody who doesn't say anything. So we take one another's hands again and call: Hey, who's looking at us? But apart from the sounds of the air and the earth and the ones we ourselves make (with our hearts, our lungs, our throats, our mouths) everything around us is hushed. Then Malente, who's walking last, suddenly starts to sing, something we've never heard before, and which perhaps doesn't really exist. How His Kingdom is mighty, ahead and behind, above and below. Something he thinks up on his own, simply inventing it as he walks along.

Hey, what's that? we call.

A song, Malente says, I'm singing a song.

Yes, we say, but why?

But Malente doesn't know that. Whenever he can't go on walking, when it's very hot, or very cold, he starts to sing, isn't it disgusting? We think we're lost and Malente sings! Us, anyway, his song disturbs, at least it's no help to us. What we want is to be getting along, who knows who'll be painted, otherwise? And we wonder what to do, so as not to be late. Should we let go of one another, should each of us go it alone? Or should we stay together here in this damp-seeming hollow? No, we won't let one another go, we think, and we stay where we are, even if, so as to keep moving, we walk in a circle. And you, Malente, don't you be singing now!

Why not? Malente asks.

So nobody will hear us.

And who's likely to hear us? Malente asks.

The people who could be here. Here in the hollow, we say. And then, a bit louder, we call: Hey, who's that creeping around us, we can hear you tapping about. But he doesn't announce himself. Till we suddenly hear something else, quite unexpected.

Till the pig, which we'd forgotten about again, but which, even if it was on the far side of a field or meadow or some plow land, was always together with us in the world and breathing along with us, though close to the ground, gives a piercing squeal, probably behind his pig house. Well, so that's over and done with! And then, as if an expectation had been lifted from all around, we at once hear voices from the hills or the vales, distant and blending, people flocking to look at the dead pig, and to turn it over on its other side and walk around it, people who, if only they'd look in our direction, would surely see us too. (For even if we can't see anything, we can still be seen, very much so!) Probably we're manifest as dark points in the wavy but generally flat countryside, which (the points) aren't rooted in the earth like trees or rocks or other natural things, but move back and forth, so that, once one has sighted them, one can follow them with one's eyes moving through the region. So that's us, being seen and becoming smaller or bigger. Anyway, nobody comes to us in the hollow, also nobody calls to us, but probably people can see us walking with soft uncertain footsteps out of the hollow and vanishing over the horizon. Then people will soon have seen enough and told themselves: O, it's only *them*! And they turn their backs on us again, to contemplate the dead pig.

Hey, we call, isn't there anybody around to take us away from here? Some helpful person who'll lead us to the pond we're expected at? May God lead him into heaven by the hand, just as he leads us away from here. Hey, is there any such person here?

But probably there's nobody here, it's the same as ever. We hear only the earth and the air and ourselves, even the pig is hushed now. And we won't hear it, even if we listen for it. So in this empty place, probably the edge of a hollow, we position ourselves in a semicircle, for, as far as we can remember with our foot-memory, we were last going downhill, therefore it *must* be a hollow. Or it's a snake pit and we just don't know it yet. Then one of us – it might be ourself – says: This wind brings rain! And immediately we draw our heads in. And we stand, unless we're quite mistaken, with our backs to the village green, for we don't want to go back there. And we join hands and softly curse and we prop one another up, because, whether from sadness or walking, our legs tremble. So that if somebody saw us from a distance standing with these legs he'd naturally think we were going to dance at any moment, but he'd be wrong. We *can't* dance at all, at least not properly. We wouldn't know which direction to step in, we'd dance past one another and farther and farther off into the remote distance, and we'd finally get lost. True, we run and crawl and chase a lot, but that doesn't mean we dance too. And even if we were able to dance, in the dark, when nobody's looking, alone on a level spot especially meant for us and kept vacant for us, why should we? Certainly, to loosen our legs we sometimes hop and kick them up, and straightaway we're misunderstood. Straightaway people call: Quick, look, now they're dancing! But that's a delusion, no, we never dance.

6

Later this wet springtime – they say whole countries are underwater – when we've been standing and stamping the earth flat for a long time in this snake hole or hollow He's led us into – we notice, yes, it's raining. At first we think it's even snowing. Naturally we'd like to find shelter, but where? There we stand, under a sky which hangs down black probably around our ears, and we feel it's a steady rain now. Our rage at the rain, that He should make it fall on us! And the smell of wet earth! What heaps of last year's leaves we hear around us now, not rustling, but rotting! The situation we're in, how clearly it shows us, at least, His Will! How we beg Him to lead us out of the hollow, if it's a hollow we're in! Instead, He leads us into a part of the hollow where the water comes up to our calves. If we go any farther this way we'll end up drowning! Turn back, turn back! But there's water behind us already too, we'll drown there as well. In any case we'll catch cold and not be fit to be painted anymore. How heartily we implore Him to save us, and He can't hear us because He's too far away! Instead, just as we get clear of the water, He sends us a dog, which isn't wanting just to sniff at us, not at all, he immediately attacks us.

Hey, Ripolus, we call – our feet in muck – there's a dog here, it seems.

Yes, there is, Ripolus says, I can hear him.

Good, we call, then hold him.

But Ripolus says he can't. He can't even see the dog, how can he hold him? Certainly he gives a shout, he grabs at him, but grabs nothing. We kick and lunge at him too, but our kicks miss.

Hey, dog, we shout, why are you attacking us?

Hey, we shout, call him off!

Instead, the dog snaps at us and hangs on to our legs. A new pain, never felt before, piercing, but quickly we get used to it. We hold one leg up in the air and thrust it back and forth, we swivel around. But the dog has sunk his teeth into us and he doesn't let go.

You dog! we scream and kick our legs about and probably swing the dog around in the air, but he doesn't give up. O Lord, we call, why don't You hear us, why don't You call for Your dogs?

All the same, He does then send us a man, we can hear his voice. Perhaps a shepherd, who speaks to the dog and calms him down and probably scratches his throat and takes his teeth out of us. And then perhaps puts him on a chain, or a leash. And says we'd irritated him and made him lose his temper and that ordinarily he's a good dog and we'd spoiled him.

Hey, is somebody there? we call and put our hands on our wounds.

Yes, the man says, I'm here.

And where exactly are you? we call, come closer, we can't see you.

Like this? the man asks, and then he's very close and we stand around him and, in spite of our pains, put our hands on his head. And feel over his face and make for ourselves a picture of him and tell ourselves he's this way or that and probably not this or that other way. Then we ask who sent him. Nobody.

But somebody surely sent him? No, he saw us walking over the field and came of his own accord.

And why didn't you come sooner? we ask, we could have been drowned.

Yes, that's true, in the pond.

So there's really a pond here?

Yes, over there.

Where?

Then the man takes us by the shoulders and turns us toward the pond and he says: There. You're lucky devils and you don't know it. Then he wants to see our wounds.

Ouch, we say when he bares them and his finger hits them, why are you doing that? Ouch!

Then he says the pain is a good sign, it shows we're still alive. And soon we'll forget about it.

But why didn't you come sooner? we ask.

Because, he says, I thought you were someone else.

Who?

Soldiers.

Soldiers! we exclaim, why?

Because you're so colorful.

Us?

Yes, from a distance.

But we aren't soldiers, we exclaim, even if we're colorful from a distance. We couldn't ever be soldiers, we'd never see the enemy. Only this one here has been a soldier, we say and take Bellejambe by the shoulders and pull him out from among us and push him toward the man.

Yessir, Bellejambe says, gunner, bangbang.

But then the gun went off backward, didn't it? we say and laugh.

Yessir, Bellejambe says, bangbang.

GERT HOFMANN

In short, even Bellejambe isn't a soldier now, he just used to be one. None of us is a soldier anymore, nor could he be. But we live in darkness, so to speak, forever. Look, we say, and pull Bellejambe back again, put him in his place, and pull up our eyelids and show the man our eyes. And tell him who we really are, and that we're going to be painted, we don't know why. But he doesn't know anything about the ravens.

In the summer, we say, while we were sitting under the cherry tree, don't you remember?

No.

Then you'll have forgotten about it.

Yes, he says, probably.

And what's your name? we ask after waiting a while to see if he might remember after all, but he doesn't, and he's meaning to tell us his name but we say: No, don't tell us.

Why not? he asks.

Because your name, we say, is only a word like any other, which, like the many other words we once knew, we'll only forget, and that only upsets us. Or it would make us feel sad.

All right, he says, so I won't tell you.

Much more important than your name, we say, is your finding us and not thinking anymore we're soldiers and taking us out of this hollow.

It's not a hollow, he says.

Not a hollow, we exclaim, then what is it?

Part of a field that belongs to me.

Well, we say, we think it's part of a hollow that belongs to you, but let's say no more of it. The main thing is for you to take us away from here to the house where the painter lives.

Why?

Because we're going to be painted.

66

But his house, the farmer says, is just over there.

To the right or to the left? we ask.

To the left.

Strange, we say, just now we were told to go to the right. Do you remember, Ripolus?

No.

No matter, we say. And to the farmer we say: So lead us over there, to the left.

If you want, the farmer says, but it isn't really necessary, it's only a little walk from here. And then, after taking us a little way in that direction, the direction we'd always wanted to go but then hadn't, because Ripolus was against it, he says that in any case the painter can't paint us as we are.

And why can't he paint us as we are? we ask as we trot behind him through the hollow.

Well, the farmer says, you can't see yourselves, but if you could . . .

Yes?

Then you'd see that he can't paint you as you are.

It doesn't matter that we can't see ourselves, we say. He'll paint us as we are.

Maybe, he says, if it's all right with him. And we carry on walking. Then he says that the painter's house by the pond can be seen ahead now, it's already looking out from among the trees. A pity you can't see it, he says.

That doesn't matter, we say, we're used to it.

A big house, he says, and if we could just turn our heads the right way we'd certainly feel its presence.

And which way should we turn our heads if we want to feel it? we ask.

There, he says, this way.

And actually, when he takes our heads in his hands and turns them the right way, we can feel the painter's house, at least we think we can. Or not, Ripolus? we ask.

Yes, Ripolus says, something's there.

Of course, we say, that's the house. And we tap our way with our sticks, full of expectation, probably toward the painter's house. Hey, we call, can't anybody see us, can't anybody hear us? Hey, we're expected here, isn't anybody here? And then, when everything stays quiet, we call: Hey, you, whom the hollow belongs to, or, as you think, the field, where have you gone? But he doesn't answer. Hey, we call and cup our hands to our ears to hear him better, but everything's quiet. So the man who owns the hollow has left us standing! But no matter, we've found the house.

Hey, Ripolus, we call.

Yes.

Where are you?

I'm here.

Then come here quickly, we say. And ask him, once he's standing beside us, if there's anybody in the house or looking out from it because he's perhaps expecting us, but Ripolus doesn't know any of these things.

You can't see if anybody's looking out? we ask.

No.

Why not?

I'm not seeing well today.

And tomorrow?

I can't tell yet.

Oh well, we say, oh well. And we ask him to take us by the hand and lead us to the house, so that we can touch it and make a picture of it for ourselves. So Ripolus takes us by the hand and leads us to the house.

Is it it? we ask, are we at the house now? And we can feel something. And we even knock on it, first with our sticks, then with our fists.

Yes, Ripolus says, I think so.

What does that mean, we ask, aren't you certain?

No, Ripolus says, not entirely.

So you can't see the house either?

No, Ripolus says, actually I can't.

Nor can we, we say. In any case that must be the house wall, there, we say and pass our sticks over what we think is the house wall. At least, we say, it sounds like a house wall.

Yes, Ripolus says, that's true.

And this, we say, is this a cross beam?

At least it sounds like one, he says. A pity that you can't see it.

The cross beam?

No, the house.

Why?

Because it's a beautiful house, Ripolus says, oh yes.

It doesn't matter that we can't see it, we say, you can describe it for us.

The whole house? Ripolus asks.

Why not, we say. And we stand there with our legs apart, sticks between our feet, and feel a bit sad. Because all the things and objects that are scattered around the world now, so random and confused, the things we sometimes run into, once had their familiar and necessary places, in the old days we knew our way around, but now ... Well, we'd better not think about that. Meanwhile Ripolus starts to describe what he might be seeing, the walls, the roof ridge, a door, but slowly, bit by bit, so we can absorb it and put it together anew for ourselves. In general, his description is probably correct, though of course not always, especially as regards details Ripolus is probably often wrong. In any case he walks alongside the house through the leaves we can hear being squashed, and he scratches the walls with his stick and describes what he can feel and scratch and perhaps see.

One thing's for sure, he says, it's a beautiful house.

Is it, we ask, high?

Yes, it's high.

And what else can you see? we ask. Can't you describe anything else?

I think, Ripolus says, that it has got windows.

So it has windows! we exclaim. And we'd like to pull the house closer, so that, even if we can't see it, at least we could smell at it.

Can one see through the windows? we ask.

Yes, Ripolus says, I think so.

And what's to be seen through the windows? we ask.

Us, Ripolus says, we're to be seen.

And what, we ask, are we doing?

We're waiting.

What for?

For somebody to notice us at last, and come out to us.

And through how many windows can we be seen?

But again Ripolus doesn't know, perhaps *two*, or three.

And can't you describe anything else for us? we ask after standing there in silence for a while.

Ah, probably it has two floors, Ripolus adds. He won't tell us anything more.

Well, we say, if it has two floors we'll all fit into it.

Do you think he'll let us all in? Slit Man asks.

Why shouldn't he let us in, if he wants to paint us? we say, and we stump up and down in front of the house.

But he doesn't want to paint us inside the house, Ripolus says, he wants to paint us in front of it.

Perhaps, Malente says, he'll paint us twice, once outside and once inside.

Nonsense, Ripolus says, he wants to paint us when we're falling.

And what if he paints us once when we're sitting and once when we're falling? Malente says.

Anyway, Bellejambe says, the house as I know it is big enough for us.

There they are, a woman's voice calls, and we hear footsteps in the gravel and somebody, probably a maid, comes to a stop in front of us and probably stands there with her arms resting on her hips, probably she's looking at us. We can catch a whiff of her breath as it passes over our foreheads and goes into our noses and eyes or eye sockets. Then she comes with her hands and takes our face and turns it toward her, so that she can see us from the front and take a good look at us.

My God, she says after looking us over for a long time.

Yes, we say, it's us, and we cross ourselves and say: The blind people, who are supposed to be painted, we've come, probably through the hollow. My God, she says once more. And then she calls high over our heads: Yes, it's the ones with the ravens.

Yes, we say and breathe toward her and then tap our way toward her too, so as to reach out for her and make for ourselves a picture of her, helped by her neck, shoulders, breasts. But she shrinks from us. She doesn't want us to touch her, she's afraid our infirmity is infectious. All the same, we can feel her in front of us, in curves, in contours, and at this moment – the birds arrive. In short low arcs they're fluttering above us and whipping the air into our faces and they caw and plunge down at us and try to settle on us, mostly, of course, on our heads.

Hey, what's this? we call.

Suddenly crows, the maid says.

Are they always here?

No, not always. We'd brought them with us.

Nonsense, we say, and we feel them flying up and down and we stand there waving our arms and we call: Go away, crows! Then everything's hushed again.

Hey, we call, are they still in the air?

No, the maid says, in a tree.

Which one?

The ash tree.

All in the same ash tree?

Yes.

Take us to it, we say. And when she's taken us to the ash tree and probably we're standing beneath it, we wave our sticks over our heads and shout: Go away, go away! And we knock on the trunk of the ash tree and chase the crows away. Then we ask her: Well, how was that?

Yes, they've gone now.

So we'd have thought. And where are they?

They're fluttering again.

Where?

Up there, above us.

In the clouds?

No, lower.

Then Slit Man suddenly asks her if she knows that these crows ate his eyes.

His eyes, the maid asks with a start.

Stop it, idiot, we say, why can't you keep quiet? Why? he exclaims, it's all right for her to know. No, we say, she needn't. And we tell the maid not to take him seriously. It wasn't long since he was slit and he still didn't know what he was saying.

Yet it was true: The crows had sat on the well and had been the last thing he saw, so he couldn't forget them and was certain they'd eaten his eyes. And then, a bit louder, with a gesture: Now, good woman, tell us – who is waiting for us in this splendid place? And loudly, so that we'll be heard inside the house too – Blessèd be the hands and fingers and eyes of him who has invited us into his house, so that he may paint us, as we were told yesterday or the day before. And may God bless the patience, we say, with which he has waited for us, but his house was hard for us to find.

They couldn't find the house, the maid shouts probably across a garden full of flowers or weeds or across a field with stubble or fruits in it. Then she says we're wet and asks if we aren't cold.

Yes.

Your hands?

Yes, our hands.

And where else?

All over.

Then put your hands in your pockets, she says.

And she takes us by the arms and leads us up a path, we notice that it's sloping upward.

Careful, she exclaims, there's a cart here, you see, I'm leading you past it now.

Well now, we say, we just thought there was something there.

So you guessed about the cart?

Not the cart, we say, but that something's there.

The higher place we're led to – the hush of the dust and stones, and over them our puffed groans, silent dogs all around us, perhaps enormous ones.

Then we ask if the sun's shining.

Yes, the sun's shining.

Thought so, we say, we can feel it, mostly on our faces. And we hold our faces up to the sun, which shines into them. It's shining on our faces, isn't it? we ask.

No.

But on our hands?

Not on them either.

And why not?

It's shining on the other side.

Of the hill?

No, of the pond.

And here?

Nothing's shining here.

Then we start to groan, to curse and stamp our feet. Why doesn't the sun shine here? Why does it shine on the other side? Why does it always shine where we are not and cannot be? And altogether everything. The blows of fate we endure, the trials and tribulations we pass through! We make too much of it, of course, for our misery isn't the worst in the world. Certainly there's much greater misery elsewhere. Then there's the misery that was and the misery still to come. All the same, we gasp and groan, so as not to be overlooked. And ask if we can be painted as we are, with our curses distorting our faces, with our wounds and our sopping clothes. And we prod our sticks into the ground and twirl around, so that the maid can see us from all sides, but she doesn't say anything. Either she doesn't want to tell us, or she's not there any more.

Hey, aren't you there anymore? we call because we can feel the gap she's left. Hey, we call, where have you gone?

Then a man who's arrived in the meantime – perhaps a gardener or a coachman – takes us by our hands that are torn by thistles and bushes and leads us back down the path again. First sand crackling under our feet, then earth, fat and moist. Yes, we've only just been taken uphill and now we're taken downhill again. Naturally we're wondering about several things. For instance: Is it still us that all this is about? If it's somebody else, who could it be?

7

And why are you so late? the gardener or coachman asks when we're down below again.

We doff our bonnets and say that unless we're mistaken we got lost, twice. And that somebody had meant to guide us, but then nobody had. So we'd walked on our own and lost our way. Ripolus had always led us to the left, instead of to the right. First to a fence, where there was no way onward, then into a hollow that was flooded and where it rained on us, we even thought it was snow. Also that we'd been attacked by at least one dog. Back there, we say and point in some direction or other. Are you the painter? we ask him.

They lost their way and got bitten and think you're the painter, the maid exclaims, she's back with us again now. And to us she says: Let's have a look at you now!

Ah, we've been looked at already, we say.

Never mind.

So we stand close together, pull our shoulders back, and keep still, and now she's in front of us, then behind us and probably looking at us.

Well, sit down now, she then says.

Where?

On the ground.

But isn't it damp?

No, here on the stones.

Good, so we sit on the stones and stretch our feet out, as best we can.

And now take your shoes off, she says.

All right, so we take our shoes off – one should take them off once a day in any case – and unwind the wrappings from our feet and stretch our legs again, so she'll see our wounds. The maid leans over us and looks at everything.

Yes, they've been bitten in the legs, she exclaims, by dogs. And us she asks: And how could you have lost the way? Because the barn we'd slept in was only a stone's throw away.

Because nobody guided us, we say.

Nobody guided them, so they lost their way, the maid exclaims. Now they're wet and bitten, he won't want to paint them like this. Bring some wood for a little fire, so they can get dry and look like something again.

But he doesn't have to paint them wet and bitten just because they're wet and bitten, the gardener exclaims – perhaps he's the knocker from this morning, even if he won't admit it. Can't he paint them unharmed and dry, even if that's what they aren't?

No, the maid says, he has to paint them as they are.

Why?

Because he has to paint what he sees.

But can't he paint *roughly* what he sees and change it a bit, improve it?

No, the maid says, that would be a lie. He has to paint *exactly* what he sees, otherwise he wouldn't have needed to send for them.

Yes, we exclaim, that's why he sent for us, to paint us as we are.

Then we hear her taking our shoes and tipping the shoes so that the water still in them will finally run out of them. (Yet he wouldn't in any case have painted the water in the shoes.) Then she wrings out our leg wrappings, they drip onto the ground. We can't tell if the wrappings are bloody from the biting. Then she rolls up our trouser legs, because our trousers are wet too, but we don't need to take them off, they'll dry in time by themselves.

Yes, they've been bitten, the maid exclaims, and she probably looks at our wounds, not touching them, though, at least we don't feel anything. Does it hurt? Yes. How much? Unbearably. Then she goes away again.

Hey, we call, where are you going? We're going to be painted today! And for a while we sit on the stones and slide around and think of our various pains, the ones in our legs and the ones in our heads. Then she comes back and stoops over us and rubs fat or grease on our wounds and rolls our trousers down again and says the pain will go away now, we just shouldn't think about it.

But if it hurts how can we help thinking about it? we ask, and we take one another's hands. Hey, we call, isn't there somebody who'll help us a bit to stand up? We can't do it, otherwise. If we'd known that nobody would help us up, we wouldn't ever have sat down. Then we wouldn't need to stand up, we'd be standing up already. Hey, we call, if somebody doesn't help us soon, we'll go away again.

But they take no notice of us, or else they're inside the house taking the fat back or bringing wood. So we stand up on our own and walk around feeling the pain, and we ask, if anybody's there to be asked, whether we'll be painted with our wounds, if that's possible. Hey, we call, is that even possible, a picture of us with wounds? But probably there's nobody there who could tell us. Later, the gardener comes back with dry branches and throws them down before us. And he starts to make a fire for us, because if we don't get dry soon we can't be painted, but will get ill, as the maid tells us when she comes back again.

First you'll cough, then lie down, and then you'll be dead, she says.

Yes, we say, God has punished us.

And then the devil will take them, the gardener says and laughs into his fire. For it's alight now, and, with hands outstretched, we go toward it, but not too close, so that we won't walk into the fire and perish in it. Instead, we have to crouch around the fire, then we feel it too, and something rises up out of us, but not smoke or fumes, which stink, it's steam, which is just damp, and slowly we get dry. And we smell the fire and hear it and hold our hands out to it, and the steam rises into our noses, and we mayn't put our feet into the flames, because then we'd be set on fire, and what then? How should he paint us if we're dry, to be sure, but, on the other hand, charred?

Have you understood that? the maid asks.

We understand, we say.

All right, the maid says. And to the gardener, who is probably standing beside her, she says: Put a few more branches on, so they'll get dry soon and won't get frozen, but only little ones. And then take them behind the trees, if they want to relieve themselves before being painted. Hey, she asks, do you want to relieve yourselves?

Probably we shall want to, we say, but not just yet.

When's that?

A bit later.

Then she goes away again. And the gardener goes away and we hear the crows and feel the wind blowing a bit, but then the wind goes away too and we're alone with the fire.

Hey, fire, we exclaim, we're alone with you. And the fire crackles. Hey, fire, we exclaim, and we're thinking: We're alone with it. And then we fart and belch a bit, so people will notice we're still here. And then, when we've been alone with the fire long enough, we call to Slit Man, just to be calling to him.

Hey, Slit Man, we call, are you still there or have we lost you?

I'm still here, he says.

Then tell us something, we say.

What about? he asks.

Old times, we say. Where did you last steal something?

In the village of Peer, he says.

And what did you steal in that village?

A foot, he says, a sacred foot.

Why?

Because at the time nobody was looking.

And then?

Then they caught me and almost strung me up, but then they reprieved me. Then they just … No, he says, I'm not going to talk about it.

Just as you wish, we say. And now? we ask.

Now I'm going to be painted.

Yes, we say, we know that. Are your feet smoking or are they only steaming?

I think they're only steaming.

Then you should shift aside a bit, we say, and let us come close to the fire too, so we can get dry at last. And then, after we've pushed him aside and stretched our legs a bit, we call: And you, Ripolus, where are you?

Here, Ripolus calls, I'm here.

And Malente, we call, are you here too?

Yes, Malente calls, I'm here.

And Bellejambe, we call, where's Bellejambe?

I'm here, Bellejambe calls.

Fine, we say, so we're all together. Or is someone missing?

No, Ripolus says, probably not.

And is anyone else here, besides ourselves?

No, Ripolus says, I don't see anyone.

And the stream, we ask, do you see the stream we're supposed to fall into?

No, Ripolus says, I don't think so.

And hear it, we ask, can you hear it?

No, Ripolus says, I can't hear it either. And you, he asks, can you hear it?

No, we say, we can't either. And then we're warm from talking and from the fire and are steaming a lot out of our smocks, and again we call: Hey, Ripolus!

Yes, he says, what now?

Ah, we say, we were going to ask if we're steaming, but we won't ask.

And we stretch our legs to get dry even more quickly, but then our feet are suddenly too warm and the steam begins to smell. Quickly we draw our feet back, so as not to get dry too fast, and call: Hey, our steam smells. Hey, Ripolus, we call, does your steam smell too?

Yes, Ripolus calls, my steam smells too.

Then we call: Watch out! The fire! but we're already in flames. At least we're smoldering and will be in flames at any moment. Help, we're smoldering! we call and lie on the ground and roll over the ground, so that our wrappings and shoes and trousers, which are probably burning or smoldering, will go out again. Help! we call, can't anyone hear us? And then we really do feel the heat. There's a burning especially around our ankles, perhaps a bit higher up too. And we roll and burn and smolder and are speechless with fright, but then we take a hold on ourselves again and go on bellowing. The maid, when she's there again, calls: Quick, pull them away! And the gardener jumps among us and pulls us to the side and probably tramples the fire out or pulls it to pieces. And they haul and drag us over the earth and knock and beat around on us, up, down, and in the middle.

Hush now, they say.

Are we really burned, we ask, or just singed?

You got a little hot.

And our trousers, we say, are they burned up or just scorched?

Your trousers, they say, are dry now.

So then he'll be able to paint us? we ask and cough because of the smoke.

Why not? they say. And they finger us and handle us to see if we're dry now, but not *too* dry, and if our shoes and doublets and smocks can still be painted as they *are*. Then they tell us, we're not hurt but are warm and dry now, and the fire is out.

Yes, we say, but now we're tired, because we've walked so far.

They're telling lies, the gardener or coachman says who's perhaps the knocker too, on account of his voice, and probably he's standing before us, they've been resting all the time. They've even been dancing, he says.

Saving your presence, we say and look in his direction, that wasn't us, it was the people before us.

And who are they supposed to be: the people before you?

The people who say they're us.

No, he says, it was you.

Well, we say, perhaps we lifted up our legs, but we didn't dance. We can't dance.

Quiet, the gardener exclaims, don't tell lies. And that of course we could dance. Proof: He'd seen it himself. You dance when you think people aren't looking, and later you won't admit it. I know you, he says.

Well, we say, if you know us, then probably you're the knocker.

Who? the man asks.

The knocker, we say, or aren't you?

No, the man says, I'm not.

Yes, we say, we'd been thinking that probably, in fact, you weren't.

Then why did you ask?

Because your voices are alike, we say. But whether or not you're alike in other ways . . .

I'm not, I'm not.

Yes, we say, we were wrong. But even so, you could have been the knocker, couldn't you?

Never, the man exclaims, me, never!

Yes, we say, probably.

And then the man who isn't the knocker suddenly flies into a rage and jumps around on the ground in front of us. Perhaps because we mistook him for the knocker, perhaps for another reason. And he shouts that it's wrong to talk with us and to be concerned with us and to let us run around, because we bring disorder into everything, thoughts, people, the air. And that we trample down everything that's in our way. Look at them, he exclaims, and probably he's pointing at us.

At once we think we might be standing among flowers and we step back, but aren't certain if we're stepping out of one lot of flowers into another. Then the gardener again: Had she – probably the maid, if that's what she is – had she seen the vegetable patch behind the house, she'd get the shock of her life. We'd stamped through it like pigs through a maize field. It was an outrage to let wretches like us go running around on the loose and tripping over their own beards. As for wanting to paint us, he just couldn't get that at all.

And where would you put them, the maid asks, if you didn't let them run around?

I'd put them…, the gardener exclaims, and probably he makes a gesture, only we don't know which one.

Yes? we ask, what is it you'd do?

Well, the gardener says, well. And he doesn't say where he'd put us. In any case we'd better be more obedient and do what we were told, we were old enough.

And if they can't find the house straightaway? the maid asks.

Then they should ask, he says, asking never hurt anybody. Really they ought to be …

But we're going to be painted! we exclaim, and we stand up tall with heads thrown back.

Ah, his wanting to paint you was just one of his whims, the gardener says, he doesn't even paint me.

He'll have a pretty good idea why he doesn't paint you, the maid says.

But us he'll paint, he even had us brought here, didn't he? we ask, and we stretch up even higher, in our partly still damp, partly singed clothes.

Don't worry, the maid says, he'll be painting you all right.

Yes, we say, he'll paint us falling over. Would he have paid for the meal otherwise?

So when did you eat? the maid asks.

This morning, we say.

Then you're hungry again?

Yes.

Then she asks if we'd like something more to eat.

Well, a knob of cheese would be good, a loaf of bread, an apple, some milk. And she: Can we eat by ourselves? We can, we can do everything. Good, then we should stay sitting there as we are now, and she'd bring something straightaway. And she really does bring bread and milk and cheese and places them on the ground, probably in the midst of us.

And the pot with the milk? she asks. Shall I put the pot into their hands, or better not?

Better not, the gardener says, they'll spill it all over themselves. Pour the milk into their mouths.

But no, she needn't, we say, she can easily put the pot into our hands. Everybody puts the pot into our hands.

We don't, the gardener says. Open your mouths, one by one, then she'll come with the milk.

All right then, we stretch out our legs, probably into the ashes, and lay our heads back and open our mouths, and then comes the pot, probably a heavy one, smelling strongly of cow shed, with the milk. And then comes the milk itself and falls through the air into our mouths. Some of the milk runs into our throats, some over our chins. Look now, the maid exclaims when she sees how we're treating her good milk and how we're spilling it on ourselves, but we simply can't drink as quickly as we're supposed to. So finally she does give us the pot and we drink the milk by ourselves and pour it into ourselves and feel it roll in big leaps down our throats into our stomachs. So the pot goes from one of us to another and we drink it empty. Then the cheese and the apples and the bread, quickly we shove them down after the milk. Then we're pulled to our feet and are led among the trees, not behind the barn, because, before we can be painted, we quickly have to empty ourselves. (We don't ask if anybody's watching.) Then we're brought out again and arranged for the picture. For this we're made to line up side by side and they walk past us. Each one of us has something wrong about him, they don't like anybody the way he is. Not one of us is good enough as he is for the painting. A bonnet is straightened, a smock is tugged around, something left hanging from our sleep is picked off, because it doesn't belong in the picture.

And the painter, has he arrived? we ask.

Soon he will, the maid says.

Will he come out to us for the painting?

No, he stays in the house.

And how will he see us, if he stays in the house?

He'll look through the window.

Is it open?

He opens it. Perhaps he'll come out to see you as well, to take a close look at you.

Will he pick at us too?

If it makes it easier for him to put you on the canvas.

Describe the canvas for us. Is it big?

Yes. Big.

Fine, we say, then he won't need to squeeze out any part of us, we'll fit into it.

Are there seven of them? the gardener asks from far off.

No, there are six.

But he wanted to paint seven.

No, the maid says, there are only six.

Well, the gardener says, that'll have to be enough.

Take them to the stream now, they'll have to line up there and walk up and down a bit.

On the bridge?

Yes.

Did you hear? the maid says, and she claps her hands, we'll make a line and walk onto the bridge.

Take hold of the arm of the person in front of you or put your hand on his shoulder.

Like this? we ask and line up and stamp our feet a bit, so we'll be able to walk better.

Yes, that's right.

And fall, we ask when we're on the bridge, should we fall now?

No, the maid says, we'll wait a bit for the falling.

The painter isn't there yet. Just keep on walking up and down, but be nice and natural.

But how can we be natural if we're not allowed to fall? At least pretend, she says.

Listen, we say, before we were stricken by our misfortune, while we were still trading in sheep and pigs and honey ...

Ah, she says, so you don't come from the poorhouse, after all?

The poorhouse came too, we say, but much later. Before that, we traded in sheep and honey and we ...

Hush, she says, there he is.

Benedictus! we call, raising our arms, and we hear a window being opened, but where? And we look in some direction or other, but probably too high up. Hey, you, we call, describe him for us. Is he smiling, or is he serious? Is he looking our way? Had he imagined us like this, or is he disappointed with us? And since one of us got lost: Will only six be enough for him?

8

The painter, who probably noticed us at once and is probably striding up and down by the probably wide-open window of his house, says – we can't hear it all – that he's always been surrounded by whole spaces full of pictures, *afflicted* by them. These spaces, he says, come to me, they come into my house. These are the spaces in which he lives, though of course there are also the other ones. How many times he's sat, especially on the long winter evenings, in the middle of those spaces and the pictures have shown him the world. More and more often now, since the slaughter at Liège, the pictures are of people dying and dead. The pictures in these spaces, now without a sky, with a high horizon, are all filled, to the limit of the frame, *gold, my good friend*, with images of people and things dying, perishing, or dead already. All *in extremis*, he says. Like these here, he adds and probably points out through the window, thus probably at us.

God's mercy upon this house! we call at once in the direction of the window, and we make a bow.

What was that? the painter asks.

They were greeting you, the good friend says.

They needn't, the painter says – he's completely absorbed in describing his interior spaces and he pays no attention to us. The sea boiling and very far off, the sky covered by a pall of smoke, glare of a fire behind soaring mountains – a memory of the far Alps – are signs that even the remoter parts of the world have been *devastated*. In the foreground, among their foothills, the last people have been gathered together to die. Even himself the painter can easily identify in the pictures of these spaces – we can hear him come to a halt in his room and draw breath – himself dying, dead already. At night he is *walled in* by these spaces with their pictures, thus also by himself. In the daytime too he only has to close his eyes and look away from other things. Then he's tempted to pick up his brush and copy the inside pictures. Yet he wonders whom he can show them to, who could endure them. Then he comes to a halt and asks: Well?

Yes, the good friend says.

And why so late?

They'd lost their way.

Have they lined up?

Yes, the good friend says, the way you wanted it.

And have they been told they have to fall, that I'll be painting them as they fall?

Yes, the good friend says, they know.

And where did you find them? the painter asks.

Not far from here, they came out of a forest, the whole place is seething with them, the good friend says. Would you have preferred to look for them yourself?

No, no, the painter says, it's fine the way it is. And probably he puts his hand on the good friend's shoulder or takes his elbow. I know it's a terrible thought, he says, but the main thing is that they really are blind.

Completely, the good friend says.

You promise me?

They're exactly as you wanted.

You looked at them?

I had them led up and down outside the house here. They really are blind.

So they move like blind people too? the painter asks, that's important, you see.

Yes, they do.

And hold their heads accordingly?

It's all as you wished, the friend says. They walk, talk, and carry themselves like blind people, yes, probably they even dream that way. (If one only knew their dreams, and if only one could paint those.) He only had to look, then he'd see for himself.

No, I don't want to look at them, the painter says after hesitating a bit, *not yet*. The mere sight of people like that had a devastating effect on him in his present state, because at once he put himself in their place. He couldn't see people who've been broken without thinking of being broken himself. So before he sees us he'd like to imagine us for a while, without actually seeing us, picture to himself how we'd be and how it'd be when he did see us. Only then, after he'd pictured and imagined us for long enough, would he look at us, that's to say, while painting us, and then he'd do it professionally and precisely. Then he'd enter into us, true, going as deeply into us as might be humanly possible. Yet, although he'd be entering into us then, he wouldn't feel close to us, so he'd be able to endure his meeting with us, this *collision*. For he was in such a state – alas, it was the case – that he couldn't allow anything to come close or excite him, except in his art. Us close – out of the question.

I know, the friend says, your health ...

My health, the painter exclaims near the window, is just the same as last year. That's to say, I still eat and drink and digest and breathe – *still*. That he didn't sleep was no secret.

But why should he talk of it? Talking of it only made him twice as sleepless.

And your eyesight, the good friend asks hesitantly, how has it been these last weeks?

My eyesight, the painter says ... Let's forget about it, he says. And them, the painter asks – he's no longer concerned with his friend – how did they go blind?

One after the other, sometimes in surprising ways, nobody knows in what order, the good friend says. Yet they say that they all went blind at the same time, in the same summer night ... It was our legend: that we'd been victims of a hot night, victims of ravens.

Ravens? the painter asks in astonishment.

Yes, the good friend says, one night. The ravens – but it could have been crows or other black birds – had suddenly settled on our shoulders and pecked our eyes out.

And people believe that?

Some do.

Well, what can one say about that? the painter says. Then comes a pause.

Good sirs, we call into the pause, we're completely blind, even if we can hear well, and we take probably one step toward them, with sticks slightly raised. We walk and move too like blind people and dream that way too, we say. And we arrange ourselves, as if we'd come to the age at which one makes oneself smaller, with outspread arms and straight backs, thus almost as if we were about to sing, probably at the window.

Is that them? the painter asks.

It's them, the friend says.

And who are they talking to? the painter asks, are they talking to one another?

No, the good friend says, they're talking to you.

Then they must be very close.

Yes, they're very close.

But I don't want them to come so close and talk to me, the painter exclaims, I'm not ready for them. Just a moment ago I didn't even know if they'd be coming, and now they're so close. They must stand farther back, please, back among those trees there.

Did you hear? You must go into the trees, so you won't be seen, the good friend calls, and he claps his hands a few times, probably out through the window.

Are there trees here then? we ask.

Yes, behind you.

We didn't know that. Are they single trees or is it a forest? we ask and tap around with our sticks.

It's a little forest.

So it's a clearing? we ask because we haven't used that word for a long time and don't want to forget it.

Yes, the good friend says, there's a clearing too.

Good, so we'll go into the clearing now, we say. And we go back among the trees, into the little forest. But we don't ask which forest we're going into, or how deep we're going into it.

Have they gone? the painter asks.

Yes, the friend says.

And what are they doing?

They're looking out from among the trees.

Can you still see them?

Yes.

Then talk to them.

What should I say?

Ask them if they can scream.

Scream? the friend asks.

Yes.

93

All right, I'll ask them, the friend says. And then, to us: Listen, he says, he wants to know if you can scream.

Scream? we say and trot up and down a bit on the edge of our forest, we don't scream much anymore.

Why not?

We haven't thought about that, we say, probably it's just the way it is. And after a few wrong steps we're suddenly standing in a sort of thicket that the friend hasn't told us about, but which is there, all the same, even if it's withered and faded, perhaps. And out of this thicket, which comes up to our knees, we speak, after trampling it down a bit, in the direction from which the painter's voice comes. While we were still trading in pigs and honey, we say, we were always honest.

Well, but don't they come from the poorhouse? the painter asks.

We've been asked that, we call from our thicket, but the poorhouse came later. Now we don't scream much anymore.

Then there's another pause.

So you want to paint them screaming? the good friend says – not to us but in the other direction.

Yes, screaming, the painter says.

And at the window he explains to his good friend that, ever since he was a child, he's been hoping to portray convincingly one day the human scream, and with a picture like that to make all the other pictures he'd painted forgettable. (Also all the pictures painted by other people.) Into this concluding and ultimate picture he'd like to put everything he had to say about the world, but so far he hadn't been able to paint a picture like that. Perhaps he'd never be able to, perhaps a picture like that is impossible. All the same, he wasn't giving up and was trying again and again to do it, in the same picture, which, as it turned out, was different each time, with the firmest intentions, naturally. But what actually resulted came from the work itself and couldn't be foreseen. Not only that the picture he'd wanted didn't result, but also that the result was often the reverse. Yet he worked hard day after day and in his head there was always the same question: if it was really worthwhile to look more precisely at this beehive or this cypress tree, this horse or this landscape.

Look at them?

So as to portray them.

And why portray them?

I don't know, the painter says, probably to capture something. Something that moves and falls and gets up again and moves onward and falls again. He didn't know why he had to capture it, or why the *scream* had to be portrayed. In any case, if he ever gets down to painting at all, he'll show the *poor people* (us!) screaming, so that they (we!) can be seen better. So that they (we), who are always being ignored, will finally be seen for once, and people will know what a human being is, what being human is about. He had marvelous views, though frightful ones, of course, into the interior of our mouths, and these views he'd take up into his portrayal. Although at the end of last winter, when, after the flooding, during which the water had risen two meters outside his house and it hadn't been heated, so that the walls had sweated whole pounds of saltpeter out ... In short: When, at the end of last winter, he'd first stumped his way out here through the last snow, he'd decided, considering his failures of last year, never to paint again. And now he was going to paint again, not just soon, but now, this very moment! Although it was so long since he'd painted from life, because the people he'd painted from life earlier had all died or been killed, and because to him it made a difference whether he painted someone who was still alive or a dead person. And, either way, of course he knew it was hopeless. Hopeless to paint the picture as it appeared in his mind, as he saw it before him, at the same time so real and so general and in its details revealing the whole, thus their (our) bodies, unmistakable, as well as what lay behind them (us), out of which they (we) briefly stepped forth to enter his picture. In short: Without hope he walks up to his easel, or up and down before it, or he sits down before it, as now, if walking has tired him. True, he always resolved to paint in a casual way, but the moment he took a brush in his hand he became as if possessed. And without much hope, as he said. Because it's quite impossible to paint the picture the way it has to be painted, terrible *and* beautiful enough. With this conviction he walks up and down before his canvas – which also worries him. For he has the impression that it will not endure what is put upon it and will soon, under the charge of the colors applied to it, simply fall to pieces, perish. Yes, it was something strange, the brush stroke, *la touche*. Thus his life was passing away as he became more and more deeply trapped in his brush strokes and felt more and more keenly that he wouldn't be able to apply them much longer. If the signs he spoke of just now are...? the good friend asks.

I won't be painting much longer, the painter exclaims, probably standing close to the window. And always he paints, so as not to waste a moment, after his long doubtings, with speed and frenzy, not thinking of much else. For when he looks around him ... So then he doesn't look around him. His excuse: that, in his case, painting, even just the thought of it, kills all thought of anything else in the world. (Although he knows that it's probably more important to live, to *survive*, than to capture life.) But he can't at the same time paint or want to paint and think of other things as well. Meanwhile, he's even doubting, of course, whether painting has any use. First comes life, which mustn't be sick or dead, then comes painting.

And the scream, what's the scream?

Well, the scream is naturally the terror, the cause of which, I willingly confess, the painter says, I haven't till now looked for patiently enough – and he starts to walk again. But he wants to look for it. And when he wants to paint the *scream*, he also wants to paint the terror, what can be seen of the terror. The way, for instance, the mouth changes when it screams, yes, that interests him. He's fascinated by the arch of the mouth cavity, the position of the teeth, the condition of the gums, the shaping of the lips, the colorings, the *dis*colorings of the palate. On the other hand, admittedly, he'd like to have painted a smile some-time, but hadn't been able to do that, either. And if he says the smile might come later, he thinks it won't come anymore now.

And why does he stress the terror so much, at the expense of everything else?

Terror? Ah, does he really do that? He doesn't feel it that way at all. What people call *terror* is the element he lives in. Certainly he doesn't want to give people a fright, far from it, and he doesn't make too much of it, either, he simply brings together what people, not wanting to think about what's ter-rible, fail to see. On the other hand the friend is right. He too sometimes wonders, while painting: In what house, in what room, among what people, for heaven's sake, would your pic-ture be in the right place, be at least *endurable*? Because at that moment he can't imagine such a place, such a wall, for the pictures he paints, *must paint*. Then he asks how things are in Ghent, in the southern provinces.

Slaughter, the good friend says.

And the slaughter in Liège?

Still going on.

You see? the painter says, and probably he puts his hands over his ears, wanting not to hear the details of the slaughter. And is probably led by the hand, by his good friend, out of the corner from which he was speaking, to the canvas, which we imagine to be empty. And he is placed before this great emptiness. Then the good friend probably places a brush in his hand, but the painter probably pushes it away and says: I can't, dear friend. But the friend won't give up, he comes again with the brush and probably even ties the brush to his hand with string, so that he won't drop it, because his fingers are gouty, or set it aside again immediately. And tells him everyone is hoping that this time he'll achieve *the scream*. Then the good friend probably puts his head out of the window and probably looks in our direction. (Looks to the edge of the forest, we're still standing on the edge of the forest.) In any case he calls to the maid, who's standing among us, and he tells her that she can lead us around now.

So he'll paint us now? we ask and rub our hands.

Yes, he will, she says.

So you'll lead us around?

Yes, she says, and she pulls us one by one out of our bushes and out from among the trees and pushes us close together, so that we'll all go onto the canvas, even if it'll quickly fall to pieces.

Hey, we call, can you see the painter now?

Yes.

Then describe him to us, we say. Is he tall and thin, with a pointed beard?

No, he hasn't got a beard.

Then he's not the one who wants to paint us.

But he's certainly tall and thin.

Then it'll be him. Then we ask: Is it light enough for painting now?

Yes, she says, light enough.

And the sun, we ask, is it shining on our faces now?

No.

On our hands then?

Not on them either.

And him, we ask, if it's him, is he looking now?

No, she says, but he'll look any moment now.

And when he looks, we ask, will we be allowed to ask him something?

Walk now, she says, walk.

But, we say, isn't there a stream, a ditch?

Yes, she says, and you'll be falling into it.

And she takes Ripolus probably by the hand and leads him probably onto the bridge, which probably crosses a stream, which we can hear murmuring. And now, she says – as we stand on the bridge and feel the wood of the bridge – do exactly as I tell you. You, she says probably to Ripolus, stretch out your stick and step onto the bridge. You go this way.

Which? Ripolus asks.

This way, she says and sets him straight. After a few steps there'll be something you won't find with your stick, and then you'll fall over it. You'll fall into the stream, it isn't deep, we'll pull you out again straightaway. But it's important that you fall.

Good, Ripolus says, I'll fall.

And you, the maid says and turns probably to Slit Man, take hold of his stick with your right hand, he'll pull you along with him. So you'll fall after him, simply fall over him. And you, she says and positions us close together, hold his stick with your left hand. You fall too.

Yes, we say, we'll fall too.

So she goes all the way down our line, walks from one to another of us and tells each of us how he's to walk and behave and stumble and fall. All the way to the last, to Malente, who has to fall too, though he won't be painted falling, but upright, just beforehand, expecting to fall.

Has he seen us now, your painter? we ask.

Perhaps he has, perhaps he hasn't, she says.

But he's looking? we ask.

He'll be looking any moment now.

Is this how he imagined us?

Yes, she says, he'll be looking any moment now.

9

No, the painter exclaims at his window, I don't want to look, I can't. He still needs some time to get used to the idea of seeing us. Poor people, he keeps on saying.

Yes, the good friend says, they are rather clumsy.

Clumsy? the painter asks, what are they doing then?

They're practicing walking.

Have they been painted before?

Not that I know.

Yes, people do fight shy of being painted, at least the simple ones do, the little people, the painter says, and he's speaking half inside his room, half out of his room. Perhaps they're obscurely afraid of the genuine thing, at least they're more honest than the others. They're afraid of being captured in a particular moment, one that's unrepeatable, of course, and then of decaying, themselves, bit by bit. Or they're afraid that later they'll find the part of them that was painted is missing. What they've got left, they think, is only the covering, the painter paints the essential thing out of them. That's why they often can't endure the sight of the picture when it's shown to them.

Yes, the good friend says, there are lots of prejudices about that.

Well, the painter says, and probably he imagines, still turned away from us, at his window, how awkward and clumsy we are as we practice walking. Cautiously, keeping close to the ground, which is very creased, we place one foot before the other on the grassy bridge and know that we'll fall at any moment. Often in the past we've fallen, to be sure, singly or together, on our hands, knees, faces. We're continuously hurting ourselves, we knock deep bloody holes in ourselves. Ripolus has a hole in his knee, Slit Man one in his elbow, there's a hole in Malente's chin, and we won't even mention ourself. Yet we never knew till now when a fall lay ahead of us and when we'd be hurt, and now that's precisely what we do know. Now we'll be falling, now, we think, and while doing so, what's more, we'll be painted. This thought, how it hampers our steps, we even creep instead of walking! Meanwhile, the painter has probably gone to his painting table and is preparing his colors: the white lead for our weathered smocks, cool gray for our bonnets, pine soot, which must be very black, for the shoes, the crows, and the branches. Sheer toil, he exclaims, getting this hard black – and probably he shows his friend the black he's obtained so laboriously. And, of course, the rose for the inside of our mouths, which has to be seen when we scream.

So should we scream now? we ask, and we're probably on the bridge.

Yes, the maid says, scream now.

Very well – and to get going we take two or three steps back and stretch our sticks out and walk forward again. While doing so we begin to scream, but, at first, with caution, softly.

Aah, we scream, *ooh* and *eeh* and *no*, and *no, don't*, and slowly we get into the swing of it, becoming more independent and noisy. And we hear how the screams escape from us and float around us, and, after they've settled over us (our shoulders, our heads) and have enveloped us for long enough, spread out across the country and settle over the neighborhood. Of course, this doesn't stop the world, but it does seem to be listening. And we open our mouths wide and close our eyes and listen to our screams, each of us to his own. And we imagine to ourselves the fields, the space around us we've been separated from since our affliction began and which we sense as a dark corridor we have to pass through, enveloped in our screams. Yet probably it isn't a dark corridor at all, but a bright expanse, a damp region lying all around us, through which we tap our way and which we fill with screams, each in his own way. With a mud hole here and there, a stream ahead of us, behind and beneath us.

Is it still frozen? we ask after we've caught our breath.

Yes, the maid says, but only at the edge. Wait, she says, I'll show you.

And she goes away, climbs down probably to the stream, and breaks off a piece of it. Then she comes up the slope again and holds it out to us.

There, she says, can you feel it?

We can feel it, we say, throw it away.

Or in another direction a probably boundless and still unplowed field beneath a sky which is always the same black for us, without sun, moon, and stars. Somewhere, probably, a farmyard from which the sound of a hammer blow comes. Also the crows in the air or in trees with probably vast leafy crests which for us exist only as a rustling. And we have the feeling that here, where we're screaming and where there's also a pond somewhere, one region of the world ends and goes over into another. And on this limit we stand, facing toward the other region, and into that region, which is put together and taken apart quite differently in the thoughts of each one of us, we scream now with gaping mouths which anyone with eyes to see can study. Malente, glass-eyed, as Ripolus thinks –

we haven't felt his face yet, and he's supposed not to have a neck either – screams especially loud, but the scream refuses to escape from him, he'll be suffocated by it if he's not careful. They say his throat is slowly closing, his rattling sounds at night give this away. When he speaks we hush and listen, for how much longer will he speak? Sometimes too we feel the air which comes out of him when he speaks, or the air he sets in motion when he draws his rattling breath. Unless we're quite mistaken, it's likely he'll become religious soon.

Then, altogether surprisingly, although we'd been waiting for it, like the sudden squeal of the pig, we fall and this is probably how it happens.

Probably Ripolus, who's leading us, strikes one of his feet against what the maid had spoken of, probably it's a stone which the gardener has rolled onto the bridge. (The maid says it won't be in the picture.) In any case, Ripolus loses his balance, starts probably to topple, probably jerks his arms upward, and falls probably backward into the stream, which, up till now, he'd only heard murmuring. Meanwhile, Slit Man probably trips over Ripolus' legs and, as he falls, pulls us along with him, for we fall too. And scream and, as we fall, reach all around us in midair for a moment and drag Bellejambe with us onto the stones, down into the stream.

Yes, that's how I'll paint them, exactly like that, the painter says to his good friend – surely he's watching us now, he's probably been looking, has seen us fall, while, in the stream we've fallen into, we're collecting ourselves and feeling for the limbs we've knocked and scrambling to our feet again in the shallow water.

Hey, you, the maid calls from high above us, have you hurt yourselves?

Yes, we call up to her.

Where?

Everywhere.

Is it bad?

We can't say yet.

Then she comes and we're led up the slope cursing and grumbling, of course (us!). What must they be up to, treating us like this, do they think we're not people?! Pushing us into a stream like that, or rather, telling us to fall into it! Once we've climbed to the top again, Ripolus is even trying to talk about our dignity, and he blurts the word out several times, but can't put it into sentences, he's too shaken. And while our voices go in and out among one another and we've hardly got our breath back, the painter, whom our fall has evidently excited and who has probably captured us in outline already, says that now he knows how he must paint us: on a bridge, over a slope, as a dark procession making a descent. And, while the maid lines us up on the path again, the painter is again at work drawing or painting, we can hear him brushing the strokes on. Whereas he'd talked a lot to begin with, he keeps silent a great deal now. And he asks the other people still in his room – we don't know how many there are – not to say anything, because he's painting now and, as he quickly explains to them, he has to scrutinize our appearance, which is only our appearance for an instant, then we'll have changed and we'd present a quite different appearance, which might cancel and contradict the previous one. And through his good friend – he doesn't speak to us himself – he directs us, please, not to fall so quickly next time, but to prolong the fall or drag it out, because it's not possible for him to capture us at such a speed. Even us, slow and clumsy as we are, we're always on the move, if not our limbs, then the looks on our faces. But at once he contradicts himself, since he admits that our *appearance*, which is easily painted, is quite superfluous, because it takes attention away from his subject, which is the constitution of the world and of human beings. And this constitution has to be caught in some other way than any direct rendering, so traps were needed. Like the length or brevity of the brush strokes, pigmentation, peculiarity of texture, the arrangement of the background, which for every picture has to be reinvented, to strengthen the figures. As to that, he'd often thought of a sort of framework which to some extent would stress what he wanted to show, even if it might look a bit artificial, yet everything in art was artifice. The trees, the clouds, plowed fields, the eye sockets, the nose, and the mouth were nothing but colors to which a form had been given, abbreviations invented each time anew, which had nothing to do with real clouds, trees, eyes, or noses, such as we see around us. Except that the colors and the forms, when they passed across from one realm to another, produced likenesses that seem deceptively real, and then we'd say: It's painted. Thank God one could paint *over* what had been painted, though one had to wait until the color was dry, or else one couldn't scratch it off.

Right, and now, my good friend, tell them to fall again, the painter says then, because he wants to capture us not posing but picking up speed, as a downward motion.

And then he goes quiet and stands probably at his easel and outlines us or fills us in, while the maid brings us closer together, pulls our bonnets farther down over our faces, and, clapping her hands, chases us back onto the bridge.

But we're going, we're going, we exclaim.

And then we walk and stumble again and scream and fall, as slowly and distinctly as we can, into the stream and lie for a while on the stones, and then we're pulled upright again. Conversely, on the canvas, as the good friend says, the superfluous and hideous blind people are rapidly being transformed into their true and beautiful and terrible picture, which will grip every one of us.

Sir, we say – after we've gone over the bridge several times, stumbled and fallen, screaming (the inside of our mouths, the terror inside our mouths!), and have been pulled dripping wet from the cold stream and up the slope for another fall – we have a few questions to ask. All this time we've been walking and falling we'd had these questions. Yes, even on our way to the pond we'd had these questions. And although the painter calls from his room, Fall! Don't ask questions, fall!, we come to a standstill on some grass, with bushes probably behind us, and look toward where we suppose the house to be, with the window and the painter. Well then: some questions.

Now what's this? the painter exclaims, they're talking, haven't I told them not to?

They're rather worn out, the good friend says.

I don't care, the painter says, they talk too much.

It's because they're worried about something.

They needn't be.

What if they have only one small question? the friend says.

All right then. What do they want?

Hey, did you hear? Just for once you may ask a question, the good friend calls – he has the advantage of being able to see our picture as well as ourselves, and he can compare us with each other in our different forms. So what do you want?

We take a few steps forward, doff our bonnets, and say, in the direction of his voice, how surprising this has all been for us. Only a moment ago we'd been walking through the countryside, and now we were suddenly being painted. Could we be told why he's painting us and what he, ourselves, and the world had to gain from it? Just see how we probably look, why would anyone want to paint that? we say and point down at ourselves, our smocks, trousers, leg wrappings, which are now, we can feel it, even damper than they were in the hollow. Shouldn't one rather be grateful if we disappeared, unpainted, as quickly as possible, we exclaim, wouldn't it be better to paint, instead, something that's not like this? For us he could do something else, help us, or console us, surely, instead of just strolling around and painting a picture of us? And then, when there's no answer, because the good friend doesn't know one and the painter, who should know one, instead of answering just goes on painting us, we ask: Why then must he paint us, isn't it enough that we exist? Or is he trying to make fun of us? Or is it (sh!) a secret? At least if everything goes well, will we be like it?

Ah, like it, is all the painter says, and probably he waves us away.

Well, the good friend says, when he sees that the painter is unwilling to speak, only very few people could judge what was really a likeness, we certainly couldn't. As for all the other questions you've asked, he says, instead of the small one you were wanting to ask – yet we'd never said we had only *one* question and a small one at that – they certainly couldn't answer them so fast, there were far too many. Isn't that so? he asks the painter.

Yes, the painter says, far too many.

And they're far too big, the friend says.

Yes, the painter says, far too big.

Very well, we say, if that's too many and they're too big, then perhaps he can answer a small one, at least, so we can see his goodwill.

Just one? the good friend asks.

Yes.

What do you think, the good friend asks the painter, would you answer one small question for them?

Well, a small one perhaps, the painter says, and probably he's gone very close to our painting now, if not crawled right inside it.

Did you hear? the good friend says, you're allowed one question, but only one. Isn't that so? he asks the painter, But the sight of us, which he endures effortlessly now that he's painting, seems only to make him want to paint, not to speak, for instead of his voice – and we're listening attentively – we hear only the scratch of his various brushes as they fill his canvas, probably more and more distinctly, with our fall, the way he wants to see it.

Good, he finally says, one then.

Did you hear? the good friend exclaims, just one, no more, and then go back to your bridge, to get on with it. Well now, he asks, what do you want to know?

Well, if we're allowed to ask only one question, then we'd like to know, we say and raise our right foot a little, then draw it over the earth ... Then we'd like to know, we say, but we notice that during the short time we've not been at the bridge and falling we've forgotten all the questions we'd wanted to ask or have asked already, we can't think of a single one. We draw our foot a few more times over the earth and our fingers over our heads and search a bit longer for the questions we wanted to ask, but we simply can't remember.

Well, the good friend exclaims, where's your question now? What do you want us to explain?

Oh, perhaps he can explain to us, we say and hope that if we take a bit of a run at it and collect everything in one long leap of a sentence and stress the sentence right, then the questions will come back. For instance, we say, can he explain to us ... But we can't think how to end the sentence. The fact is: We simply don't want to know anymore why the painter is painting us. All we want to know is whether he'll be finished soon. Sorry, we say, but no question occurs to us at the moment. And we put our bonnets back on. It seems, we say, that at the moment we have no question. So we'd rather not ask anything now, later perhaps, when something occurs to us again.

All right, the good friend says, then go back to your bridge, if you haven't got any questions.

Yes, we say, we'll go back again now.

And we're led by the maid, who has probably been standing among us all this time – so our breath was passing through her hair – but who also hasn't told us what we wanted to ask the painter, back to the bridge, where we . . .

Well, we just scream and fall again, more or less as they wish, and scramble to our feet again and crawl up the slope, and the painter says: That's right, and he goes on painting us. With new strength, as he says to his good friend, for he hadn't been able to paint all winter, but that was over now, as one could see, the dead were coming to life again. Or he says that if it goes on like this, then his blind people, even though he's showing them as horrors, must soon be worth five hundred talers to any shopkeeper with eyes in his head, God Almighty! When one thinks, he says, that in a few weeks we'll be able to see the trees blossoming, whereas they, he says pointing probably at us, all they see is blackness. And he's convinced that as a painter he'll never be or produce anything significant, distinctly he feels this to be so. Supposing everything had been different, the times, his character, circumstances, the world's and his own, yes, then perhaps something might have come of it, but the way things are, the way things are . . . In spite of all the paintings he'd done, everything still remained to be done, but he had it all in his head. As fate would have it, he hadn't yet been able to paint the pictures that were in his head, but perhaps that would come in time. Yes, he then says, at about this time last year he'd begun to work with just as much zest, but what had become of that year? And then, after a few summary brush strokes, perhaps over a painted sky or a painted field: In a biggish composition that was leaning unfinished against his bedroom wall, he'd begun an avenue of red and white blossoming chestnut trees flecked with sunlight. As well as many pencil studies for other paintings, of course: a burning bridge with collapsing towers and smoking roofs in Ghent, and a pretty view of Antwerp in ruins, both from memory, frontal views. And now tell them to fall again, he exclaims, and the maid lines us up again.

10

We'd been thinking our time with the painter by the pond would be short, but our visit lasts quite a long time. Again and again we have to scream and fall and walk over the bridge. (Because the painter wants to bring out the fine points, easily overlooked, of the looks on our faces and our movements, our faltering and gaping.) Since the sun is actually shining now, and since our comings and goings have been many, our day is becoming a hot one. We pull open our smocks, but then have to close them, because, as the good friend calls to us from the window, we have to be captured and passed down with buttoned and not open smocks. Also the wrappings around our legs – we don't know if he's painting them – we'd like to unwind them, but then two voices call from the window at the same time: No, don't unwind them, don't unwind them, leave everything as it is.

The bonnets, too? the maid asks.

Yes, the bonnets too.

And if they're sweating?

That doesn't matter.

Naturally we go on hoping for a long time that we'll remember *the question* we wanted to ask, but we hope in vain. For a while we go on looking for it, then we forget about it. So we'll probably never know why, on this day, we're being painted.

We'll never know whether we're a likeness (or how much of one we are), but perhaps that's not important. At least the painter is content.

Just look, he keeps saying to his good friend.

Yes, the friend says, it's coming along.

The eyes, do you see their eyes?

Yes, I do, precisely.

Isn't that it? the painter says, and he's very excited now by the sight of us (the sight of us on the bridge and on the canvas). Which, as he exclaims again and again, does wondrously sum up the ways of the world and the fate of man, but the good friend, who may have a different idea of these ways and this fate, or who might be horrified, only says, each time: If you think so – and he doesn't argue. Nor do we know what the sight of us sums up for the painter, we just go on saying: All right, now we'll fall, all right, time to fall. And let ourselves be led back to the bridge, stumble, scream, and fall. But after the falling, during which we've torn all our clothes bit by bit and have begun to bleed all over, it's not the maid who comes now, it's the gardener who picks us up from the stones. And he has to strain every muscle to pull us up the slope again, because, naturally, we're completely worn out, completely out of breath. Or else he (the gardener), who leaps around us in his nasty mood, may already be standing in the stream bed and waiting for us, head tilted back, anticipating our fall. (The maid, for whom we've called several times, has probably left the scene, perhaps she's in a cow shed, perhaps after a short sit she came from the cow shed again, to carry a pail past us, if that was her.) Of course, we're at the end of our tether too, so is the gardener, probably, but we can't leave the scene yet, we're still being painted. The painter is the only person who isn't worn out, in spite of his many infirmities (stomach, eyes, head), he never stops painting us, for now he's completely at home with the sight of us, while his good friend, probably looking over his shoulder, calls out to him over and over again how *excellent* he finds what's being painted, and that if the painter means to paint a masterpiece he only has to go on like this. Until we suddenly feel we're not needed anymore, until somebody even shouts this to us. Somebody who'd been silent till now shouts it from the window.

Stop now, he shouts, take them away.

So he doesn't need them anymore? the gardener asks.

No.

Did you hear that? the gardener says to us, you can go now, he doesn't need you anymore.

Us? we ask, and we stand there.

Yes, who do you think?

And where are we supposed to go? we ask.

Home.

We can't, we exclaim at once.

Why not?

Because we don't live hereabouts, we're only passing through, we say and point to the neighborhood we've passed through.

Then go where you do live.

We can't do that either, we say, we're always passing through, everywhere.

Quiet, the gardener exclaims, you're always contradicting. It upsets everything, all this contradiction.

All right, we say, so we'll be quiet, so we'll go away.

And nobody holds us back, either, as we walk, not pushed, a few steps in a direction we've probably never gone in before.

All right, we say as we pass the house probably for the last time, we'll go now. We won't be a burden to you anymore, we call quickly over our shoulder.

And how will you do that? the gardener asks – probably he followed us a little way – not be a burden to us anymore?

And with the house behind us, making a grand gesture to include the countryside we've been incessantly imagining ever since we arrived, but which, for the gardener, for the maid, for the painter and his good friend, is probably quite different, we call: We're going, but we don't say where we'll be going or for how long we'll be gone or if we'll come back one day or if we'll have disappeared forever. We detest the gardener at the house by the pond, we detest the whole neighborhood, because something here is coming to an end, or it should be.

And where are you going? the gardener asks – from the very start he's only made things difficult for us. And we think for a while and say: Over there, and we point high over the ground, far into the distance.

You can't go there, the gardener says, that's where everything stops.

No matter, we say, we already knew that, but it's where we'll go. And we point in another direction and call: You hear, Ripolus? That way, let's go!

But I don't see much in that direction, Ripolus says.

Then what do you see?

Nothing, actually.

No matter, we say once more because the words are still warm. And we grope for Slit Man's hand, who's walking in front of us, and for Malente's, who's walking behind us. What's more, we find the two hands and press or squash them and follow Ripolus, first one way, then another, and then to the side, first this side, then the other. Then Ripolus stops and doesn't know where to go. We stop too.

You can't go anywhere, the gardener says – perhaps he's moved a fair distance from us in the meantime – you'll have to stay where you are. And wait until somebody takes you away, but I'm not going to.

We wouldn't even have wanted you to, we exclaim.

No, he exclaims, I'm not going to. And he turns probably in some direction or other which we haven't foreseen and probably goes away. We follow him with our heads turning to listen for his footsteps and tell ourselves: Good riddance. And we imagine the interval between us increasing and the mere distance making him steadily smaller and smaller, and he no longer sees us and finally he's no more.

So we'll just wait until somebody else comes, we call to him quickly, but most likely he can't hear, at least he doesn't call back. So we'll just wait, we're thinking. And we crowd together and drag our feet a bit this way and that and stump around one another a bit, all keeping step. And finally we're all standing like a dense clump, all on the same spot, and we grumble and moan again, just as we'd moaned and grumbled on the path going uphill, except that now it's a slower and more feeble grumbling. Possibly too we take a nap, upright, propping one another up. Or we think about something, call something up from down inside us, perhaps a memory, or something we think is a memory. And then, after we've stood around and moaned long enough, it starts to rain again. When Slit Man hears the rain he starts to curse, but Malente is almost proud of the rain, as if he'd made it. A rain coming as if through a fine sieve, which, it occurs to us, we'd probably have called in earlier times a drizzle, and so distinguished it from all other kinds of rain, but does the word still exist?

Hey, Ripolus, we call.

Yes, Ripolus says, I'm still here.

And where are you? we ask.

Here.

Good, we say, then listen, we have a question.

Fine, Ripolus says, I'm listening.

Right: What's falling now? we ask and hold him by the elbow.

Falling? Ripolus asks, has somebody fallen down?

Idiot, we say, on us, on us, falling on us. Isn't that a drizzle?

A what?

Or isn't it?

But Ripolus can't remember, he doesn't know the word anymore, even the thought that he might have forgotten it doesn't occur to him. No, he says, the word doesn't exist, never has existed.

But to us, if we remember rightly, we say, it seems ...

Doesn't exist, Ripolus exclaims, doesn't exist!

In short: At this point in time – soon to be our last – we doff our bonnets, to let the elements refresh us a bit up top. And we hold our faces up to the sky – the wild ducks overhead are probably flying back north again – hold them into the fine rain, the thin wind.

Then a voice says: Come on now.

Hey, we call, is somebody there?

Yes, the voice says, somebody's here.

How's that?

Always was.

And how long still?

Yes, over here, by the bush.

We tap our way across. Is there a bush here?

Yes, there's a bush.

If the ...

Bush?

No.

The speaker?

Here then?

No.

Here?

That's right. And he takes us firmly by our hands and draws us across a meadow, which could also be a field or a pasture, so that we can't even try to imagine what's beneath us, but something's there. Also we don't know which clouds we're turning our backs on or which are ahead of us. Quickly along under these clouds, until we've gone far enough. Until we're pushed into a barn – at first we think it's a big cupboard – and the rain goes away again, and a door is slammed shut behind us, of course. Then the wind around us goes away too, the rattle of leaves in the trees.

Hey, we call, what have you pushed us into?

Sleep now, the voice says, it's raining.

Yes, we're thinking, and it'll snow. And we stand there and put our bonnets back on and cock our heads up high, because that way we hear better, but we don't hear anything. We only feel the air, how quietly it stands around us, the roof, the darkness. Darkness that we only suppose to be there and of which we can't tell if it's the night's or the barn's. (We'd like it to be the night's, then we'd feel more protected, or certainly less exposed.) In the hush that now comes we imagine the snow descending on us from very high up and how we sink down into this snow, legs, shoulders, heads. Then we think: Yes, it's night, the real one, not just the other. And we hope that nobody will come and talk to us about the stars. For who knows, perhaps there are stars today, or a rotten tree is glowing and it's only a question of time before somebody will talk to us about it. Then it occurs to us: But how can it be night, we haven't had anything to eat! All we've done is walk and fall, won't anyone give us food and drink? And we put out fists to our forehead and stay like that for a while. This hush around us! (The hush of things that don't move and probably never will move, whatever happens.) Then we grip our sticks more tightly – what else should we do? – and since we've stood long enough we walk a few steps softly over the earth of the Lord and through the darkness of the Lord and through the barn, the *rubbish pit* of the Lord, into which we've been pushed. For we begin to shiver and shake if we haven't been moving for a long time. Move, we say at daybreak, and off we march. And in our ears we have the shuffling of our feet over His ground. And in a single day we walk through three villages, sometimes even four. Or at least we think we're walking through four villages, but actually we'll be walking around in the first village all the time. Or else they capture us and put us in the sun, where we have to weave baskets. In any case, we move a lot, also before and after the weaving, so the shaking won't come up, won't even grope around for us. In the evening we're much too tired even to shake. Anyway, after a few steps we come up against a lath wall. Which, no doubt about it, is an old acquaintance.

Hey, there's a lath wall here, we call at the end of this Lazarus day of ours or thereabouts, and we knock on the wall. Hey, what have you pushed us into, we know this already.

What do we know already? Bellejambe asks.

All this.

And how come we know it? Bellejambe asks.

Because we've been here before.

Me too? he asks.

Yes, you too.

And when do you think we were here? Bellejambe asks.

Probably this morning.

Me too?

Yes, we say, you too. But perhaps it was another morning, we aren't quite sure. Can't you remember?

No, Bellejambe says, you've been dreaming.

Yes, we say, we've been dreaming, but of something else. And we tell him how somebody woke us up, took us out of our dream. Do you remember somebody waking us up?

No, Bellejambe says, not me.

But he did. We were under the earth already, only one leg was still hanging outside. And that wouldn't have been there much longer, because snow was falling on it. But then he knocked on the door and took us out again.

Who?

The knocker, we say. And after we'd been stood back up on our feet somewhere in this neighborhood, we say and grope around with our stick, we were led outside and to the table, where the bowls were. Which were all for us to eat from and which we could empty.

Not me, Bellejambe says.

Not you?

No, not me.

So you mean you've forgotten it all? we ask and know exactly what he's thinking. Like us, we think, exactly like us! How often we tell ourselves: Let's just go to sleep! – and forget that we're already asleep. Or we think we're dreaming while we're really awake and – we'd forgotten it – eating or walking.

I didn't empty anything, Bellejambe says.

Yes, you did, we say, you've forgotten, that's all.

Have you forgotten the child too, who wouldn't believe us? What child?

The one who took us behind the barn.

And what didn't he believe about us?

That we're blind.

He wouldn't believe I was, either?

That's right.

He didn't believe I was blind! Bellejambe exclaims and strikes the ground with his stick.

No, he didn't.

And why not?

Because you kept on looking in his direction when he said things. Do you remember now? we ask.

No, Bellejambe says, you've dreamed it.

All right, we say, and we give up and step aside a bit and wonder if a person who remembers so little is still alive. If what was so in the morning ceases to be so in the evening. If that's the case, then it's unfortunately certain that many of us must be dead already.

Hey, Bellejambe, we call, why don't you say anything? Are you dead?

No, Bellejambe says, not yet.

So you can still hear us?

Yes, he says, you've dreamed it.

Yes, we say, but then somebody woke us up.

Not me he didn't, Bellejambe says, not me.

Well, we think, at least we're back again where we probably started, probably this morning, after a long and strenuous, but uneventful and boring walk. At least that's how it feels here. Hey, we call, is anybody else here, or are we alone?

And we stoop and hunch our back and are on the verge of collapse, or sinking into the ground almost, that's how far gone we are. But then we only fall to our knees and ask for enlightenment. Lord, we think or call, Thou knowest that for a long time we haven't seen Thy earth, which Thou hast established also for us, grant us that we too, we too … But we don't know how to go on, because it's always hard for us to complain and suffer consecutively for a long time.

Ripolus, we call and stand up again and walk up and down, because we don't want to get stuck in one place.

Yes, Ripolus says, what do you want?

We want! we call.

What you want is nothing, Ripolus asks, isn't that it?

No, we say, we want to know something. We want to know if you think somebody's here, looking at us.

Yes, Ripolus says, if only one knew whether it's dark.

And whether, Malente says, dark or light, anybody at all is looking.

Do you think it's dark? we ask.

Who could be looking? Bellejambe exclaims.

I don't think anybody's looking, Slit Man says – we'll certainly push him into a ditch soon.

And why not? we ask.

Because there's nobody here who could see, Slit Man says, otherwise he'd announce himself.

Hey, is anybody here? we call. But it's true, nobody announces himself.

And then, when nobody has announced himself for long enough, we reach forward with our sticks and tap along the lath wall, first Ripolus, then the rest of us. Later, to make even more sure of it, we also touch it with our fingertips. The lath wall is rough and cold and we scratch at it and knock on it. And feel cracks in it, through which fingers can be put, or fingertips at least. Until we come to a corner, a barn corner. A corner, at least a corner! We stop, draw breath, fill the corner up. And stay in the corner for a while, establish ourselves in it.

Hey, we call, isn't there anybody here?

And then, after hesitating a bit, then leaving the corner and the lath wall as well, we go deeper into the interior of the barn and hit on straw. Straw, of course, there had to be straw, we'd smelled straw! Also there'll be animals here perhaps, only they're not announcing themselves. Perhaps if we go a bit farther like this we'll even hit on animals, run into them. Probably they'll have lain down already and settled into the positions in which they spend the night, thus close to the ground. Anyway we smell not only straw, but also animals. But we smell and feel ourselves too. On top we smell like damp, down below it's like fire and dust, and in the middle, we smell ... Well, we're alive, all the same. Then suddenly we start to laugh, we astonish ourselves. For a long time we stand up to our knees in the straw and can feel ourselves laughing, the shoulders, the throat, the belly. Even our legs, which mostly are hushed, join in the laughter. At first we laugh softly and each by himself, each in his own direction, then loud, in chorus, all of us together. And we feel the tears running down our cheeks and throats, into our shirts.

All right, we call, is anybody here? For the last time: yes or no?

No, a voice says outside the barn.

Aha, we say, so we weren't mistaken?

Yes, you were, the voice says, because he's going now.

And us, we ask, have you shut us in?

Yes.

Why?

So you won't hurt yourselves in the darkness.

In which darkness, we ask, the barn's or the night's?

The night's.

So it's night again, we exclaim. And by our voices we can tell: Yes, it's night, it must be night. Because it has a different sound from day when one calls into it, even inside a barn.

We are in a barn, aren't we, or...? we ask.

Yes, in a barn.

The same one as last night? we ask.

Yes, the same one.

Ah, we say, we thought so. Then you'll be the knocker who came this morning?

Yes, the knocker says, this morning.

We ask: Why did you wake us up?

And the knocker says: Because you were going to be painted.

Curse it, we say, couldn't you have waited? We'd almost disappeared.

Yes, the knocker says, woken up.

And we, the people in the middle of the picture, we say: So are we painted?

And the knocker, going quickly on his way: Yes, you're painted.

Afterword

MICHAEL HOFMANN

As a writer, my father Gert Hofmann (1931–1993) came out of drama, in particular that rather spectral thing, radio drama (where the standing boast was that they had better visuals than TV: well, who would argue with that).

Once I can get people talking, he sometimes said later, I'm away. We tended to live in small or middle-sized towns, and mostly he made his own entertainment, and ours with it: he would read aloud to us some evenings, sometimes his own works, mostly others', Thomas Mann and Kafka, but also Hofmannsthal, Musil, Gogol. One of the few great theatrical experiences of his life – if it even happened, but I'm inclined to think it did – was a visit to Paris in the 50s, to catch the first run of Beckett's *En attendant Godot*. (Among very many other things, *The Parable of the Blind* is clearly a version of *Godot*: the outlandish preparation, the bleak *tour* of the equally bleak *horizon*, the big no-show, the equally dismal scene before and after. "All right, we call, is anybody here? For the last time: yes or no?")

In the 60s and 70s, then, in his own thirties and forties, he wrote radio plays. We were living outside Germany at the time, his children collated the scripts from the different carbons, he sent them off, later got word of an acceptance and maybe a transmission or a repeat date. It all seemed remote, thankless, a little theoretical, offshore; at the most my parents might open a bottle of wine. There was little question of our actually being able to *hear* any of the works being broadcast. Still, others did, and my father won prizes for them, among them the most coveted of German radio prizes, the one given under the auspices of the German War Blind. He didn't write novels until his fifties. A book, too, felt like something to be consigned to the (air)waves.

On the cover of one of the annual program catalogs for one of Germany's many federal broadcasters, I saw a photograph once of a group of delightfully civilian-looking actors (look, no costumes!) clustered round a microphone suspended from the ceiling, one of them perhaps with a desk or tray in front of him, a little box of tricks, a bell, a whistle, a half coconut shell: the sound effects man. That was all you needed, and in a sense, the less the better. Then there was something called *Kunstkopf*, "art-head" or "artificial head," a way of engineering binaural reception within the radio listener's head, by means probably of headphones. Later on, something like that could become the basis for a novel as well, as here, where amid the prevailing uncertainty about everything, the subjects have a way of being *pierced* by sounds. They may not know where they are, or understand what is being done to them, but they can at least give or repeat a direction (for instance, to the hapless Ripolus), left or right, up or down, forward or back. The human skull – the reader's, or if that was not forthcoming, then just his own – was my father's sounding-board. You might think of that while reading *The Parable of the Blind*.

My father had two overriding themes in his work: cruelty and art. Children might come into either – their joyful and unbounded capacity to do and suffer harm, and their untrained and unpredictable creativity. (In his own life, childhood, the years from 8 to 14, coincided with the War. How was he to know the difference?) Just five pages into the present book, a child is – perfectly reasonably – poking its fingers into the blind men's eyes:

And if I press a bit?
No, we say, you mustn't press.
But you don't see anything anyway.
All the same, we say, you mustn't press.

Often there were choruses of children's voices commenting or disrupting the action of a play. Angelic voices chanted terrible or inapplicable things. Accordingly, when my father took up prose, he sometimes slipped into the we-form, and this came to be where the narrative perspective was sited in some of his books. An I-plus-one, or a sinister small town, or a defeated and discredited fatherland speaks, or sometimes elements of all three. In *Our Conquest* (of 1987), in *Veilchenfeld* (1986 – and never in English, but *Notre Philosophe* in French), in *The Parable of the Blind* (1985 – Christopher Middleton's translation came out the following year). A strangely elastic, unlocatable, impersonal we-form, something that doesn't count its lumps, and to whom the sweetest flesh isn't that which covers its own ribs; something peripheral and defensive, always alert to threat or pain. Something that, when pushed, shrinks, even into the singular: "our cap," "our suit," even "ourself." Something that also remains riven, in spite of grammar, or onion-layered, so that the remaining five have it in for Slit Man, the convict and thief in their midst – though one wouldn't trust them with Ripolus or Bellejambe or Malente either, which leaves just the two anonymous ones in the middle, the engine-room, so to speak: the "we" in the "we."

The discourse – silly word, but I don't know what else to call it! – is served by a style that is somehow all knees and elbows. And here I must applaud Christopher Middleton's translation, which leaves things as rough and strange as he finds them:

> The morning breeze is waiting out there, it blows toward us.

> Hey, what's this? we call.
> Suddenly crows, the maid says.

> Then we start to groan, to curse and stamp our feet. Why doesn't the sun shine here? Why does it shine on the other side? Why does it always shine where we are not and cannot be? And altogether everything. (p. 87)

Every move is an ontological pratfall, a philosophical banana peel. My father's preference and predilections both were for work that was graphic, rather than painterly (he admired and collected two contemporary artists: the Spaniard Jorge Castillo and the Scot Pat Douthwaite, both masters of an idiosyncratic line). Not for him the art of filling in; the studio assistants spreading a thing into its four corners; the days when he was painting sky (as was said of Caspar David Friedrich) being the ones when he couldn't be spoken to. No, it's a matter of lines, and often of rude lines, unanswerable lines, the ones that go into the third or fourth or fifth dimension, the ones that make directly for depth and darkness. The unsettling modifier "probably" affords a temporary solution, but only a temporary one: probably, probably, probably. The preferred form of question, from the very beginning, is the one that's hardest to answer: why.

> Painted? we ask.
> Yes, painted.
> And why are we going to be painted?

(Later on, they turn the question on Slit Man: "And why are you going to be painted?" He of course doesn't know any more than the knocker.)

The depleted world of the blind is continually cruel, unpredictable, mysterious. They are made to deal with imponderables like shadows and self-portraits; wish they could have been fitted with "a nozzle or sucker, not necessarily a long one" so that they could bring up items and sniff them, but also so that they could themselves be more easily recognized from a distance (absurdly, they are allegedly mistaken for soldiers at one stage); speak of "our friends the cripples"; find that not only is the world thin, lacking in spice and interest and beauty, but also that their vocabulary is dwindling, which in turn causes them to wonder whether "the thing is still behind the word" or has it not possibly atrophied as well. A whole entropic world is built up – spun off – from a lack or lacks, a world that quite literally comes up and bites them ("A new pain, never felt before, piercing, but quickly we get used to it"), all the while "they say whole countries are underwater" and fresh atrocities are being committed in Ghent and stale ones in Liege. (It might be worth noting that 1568, the year Brueghel – probably – painted the eponymous picture, is also the year of the beginning of the Eighty Years' War between Catholic Spain and Protestant Holland.) Their world, which is the world of the book, which is also our world of recurring catastrophe and unabating war, is only ever half a step (if that) away from morbidity, from cruelty, from darkness. Why, the first sentence is barely underway before it's interrupted by a groan of complaint, of *taedium vitae*, of enough already, "yet another new day!" Even such an apparently fanciful or ornamental thing as the enmity between the blind of the earth and the birds of the air turns out to be dreadfully well-founded:

> And why then did they peck your eyes out?
> Because we killed their young.
> And why did you kill their young?
> We'd had enough of their noise, we say, at least we thought we had.

The exchange is with the child, and seems designed, at least in part, to intimidate it. This is a world without a smidgeon of innocence anywhere.

And now it is to be painted. Absent religion, art is our principal remedy for reality and mortality, only the blind of course don't really stand to benefit much:

> So are we painted?
> And the knocker, going quickly on his way: Yes, you're painted.

Meanwhile, the painter – the name Brueghel doesn't appear anywhere – only makes things worse. He refuses to leave the house, paints – probably – through the window, deals with his subjects through intermediaries (the "good friend") and menials. He doesn't answer their questions. He suborns them, insists on their blindness, needs to have it confirmed that their likenesses have never been painted before. Ironically, his eyesight seems to be not much better than theirs. He is at once hard-headed and soft-headed. "He couldn't see people who've been broken without thinking of being broken himself" – which reminds me of Saul Bellow in the account of his friend John Berryman, unable to browse the newspaper, because he felt obliged to identify himself with everyone in it, "including the corpses, pal." ("Dream Song # 53") He is consumed by his own anxieties, and cloaks them in those of his craft. He seems every bit a modern painter, a *maudit*, from after 1800 or 1830, or whenever the arts were finally and irrevocably confirmed as neurasthenic: I know my father based him partly on Francis Bacon (the interviews with David Sylvester, the screaming Popes, the Eadweard Muybridge serial photographs analyzing movement, "because he wants to capture us not posing but picking up speed, as a downward motion"), perhaps also Goya, Van Gogh, Munch (who compounded his own blacks himself, as our man here does, "sheer toil, he exclaims, getting this hard black.")

In the end, the whole thing is the model of a useless transaction. The blind, put through it and degraded, but perhaps not much worse than usual; is their sitting – their falling and screaming – that much worse than their defecating – because they have been promised privacy – in full view of everyone on the village green? The painter, briefly exalted by something he has done, ("The eyes, do you see their eyes?") but still on a grimly downward trajectory himself, a prey to his doubts and fears and hypochondrias even as he speculates that what he has made "must soon be worth five hundred talers to any shopkeeper with eyes in his head, God Almighty!". The picture, in the sardonic commentary of the sitters, certain to "quickly fall to pieces," which is something they know something about. The world, as usual, quite unaffected, set in its ways, going to hell in a handcart.

And my father's triumph: to have seen all this and brought it back to the reader with his typical patience, humor and imagination.

MICHAEL HOFMANN

GERT HOFMANN was born in Limbach, Germany, in 1931. For many years a professor of literature in Europe and the United States, he was also the author of numerous radio plays and a singular series of prose works, including the novels *The Spectacle at the Tower, Our Conquest, Before the Rainy Season, The Film Explainer, Luck*, and *Lichtenberg and the Little Flower Girl*, as well as a collection of stories, *Balzac's Horse*. Hofmann died in Erding, near Munich, in 1993.

CHRISTOPHER MIDDLETON was born in Truro, Cornwall, in 1926. He was an acclaimed poet and translator. He published translations of Robert Walser, Nietzsche, Hölderlin, Goethe, and many others. His last books included *A Company of Ghosts, Just Look at the Dancers, Frescoes with Graffiti & Forty Days in the Calypso Saloon, Nobody's Ezekiel*, and *Loose Cannons: Selected Prose*. Middleton died in Texas in 2015.

MICHAEL HOFMANN, the son of Gert Hofmann, was born in Freiburg, West Germany, in 1957. He is the author of four books of poems, *Nights in the Iron Hotel, Acrimony, Corona, Corona*, and *Approximately Nowhere*, and two collections of essays, *Behind the Lines* and *Where Have You Been?*, as well as numerous translations from German, including works by Joseph Roth, Peter Stamm, Gottfried Benn, Franz Kafka, and Hans Fallada. His *Selected Poems* were published in 2008.